# DOCTOR DOLITTLE'S
# RETURN

# DOCTOR DOLITTLE'S

# RETURN

## by HUGH LOFTING

Illustrated by the Author

RED FOX

A Red Fox Book
Published by Random House Children's Books
20 Vauxhall Bridge Road, London SW1V 2SA
A division of Random House UK Ltd

London Melbourne Sydney Auckland
Johannesburg and agencies throughout the world

First published in Great Britain by Jonathan Cape 1933

Red Fox revised edition 1992

Set in Century Schoolbook
Typeset by JH Graphics Ltd, Reading

Printed and bound in Great Britain by
Cox & Wyman Ltd, Reading, Berkshire

ISBN 0 09 988070 9

*To You*
  *Hopeful    Huntress,
Sturdy   Swimmer,   Best
Companion of the Field,
the   Road   and   Stream,
True  Philosopher,  Most
Beautiful   of   Cocker
Spaniels
  I Dedicate*
                *This Book*

# Contents

# Illustrations

# PART I

# Chapter One
## WAITING!

**D**OCTOR DOLITTLE had now been in the Moon for a little over a year. During that time I had been in charge of his household at Puddleby-on-the-Marsh. Of course a boy of my age could not take the great man's place — nobody could, for that matter. But I did my best.

At the beginning it was not easy. We were all so anxious and worried about John Dolittle. We did not seem to be able to keep our minds on anything but that he was still in the Moon and what might be happening to him. So it was in our talking too: no matter what we started to discuss or chat about, our conversation always ended on the same question.

Yet I do not know what I would have done if it had not been for the animals. Ah, those animals of John Dolittle's! Dab-Dab the duck, the careful housekeeper who spent her life looking after others — even if she did it scolding them most of the time; Jip the dog, brave, generous, happy-go-lucky sportsman, always ready for a good scrap, a good story, a good country walk or a good sleep; Too-Too the owl, silent and mysterious, with ears

that could hear a pin drop in the snow, a lightning
calculator — you never knew what he was thinking about — but he seemed to guess things, to *feel*
them, witch-like, before they happened; dear, old,
clumsy Gub-Gub the pig, always in hot water,
taking himself very seriously, for ever treading
on somebody's toes but providing the world with
lots of fun; Whitey the white mouse, a gossip, very
well-behaved, very clean and neat, inquisitive,
taking in life every moment and finding it full of
interest: no one unable to talk the language of
birds and beasts will ever understand how
thoughtful and helpful they could be.

Of course, it must not be forgotten that they
were very experienced. Never before, I suppose,
has a group of animals been gathered under
one roof that had seen so much, gone to so many
places and done so many things with human
beings. This made it possible for them to understand the feelings of people, just knowing their
language made it possible for John Dolittle
and myself to understand them and their
troubles.

Although I tried hard not to show it, they all
knew how miserable I felt about having left the
Doctor in the Moon, and they did their best to
cheer me up. Dab-Dab formed a regular school
programme for me for what she called an
'advanced course in animal languages.' Each
night, when there was no Moon to be watched —
or when it was cloudy — she told one of the
household to play the part of teacher for me. And
in this way I was not only able to keep up my Pig-
gish, Owlish, Duckish, Mouser languages and the

rest, but I improved a great deal upon what I already knew. I came to understand and use a great many tricky little niceties of meaning which I had never known before.

Of this Gub-Gub the pig, Too-Too the owl, the white mouse and the others of the Doctor's household were very proud. They said that if I kept on at that rate it would not be long before I could talk their different tongues as well as John Dolittle, the greatest naturalist of all time. Of course I could never quite believe that; but it encouraged me a lot just the same.

One who did a great deal to cheer us up in those long days and nights was Cheapside, the London sparrow. Born and brought up in the struggle and strife of a big city, he would not, could not, be beaten by any misfortune. It was not that he did not know and feel the danger the Doctor was in as much as any of us. But it was part of his character always to look on the bright side of things. He was not with us all the time. He had to pop over (as he called it) to London every once in a while, to see his wife, Becky, and his hundreds of children, cousins and aunts who picked up a living around the cab-ranks near St Paul's Cathedral and the Royal Exchange.

From these relations he would bring us back all the gossip of the big city, such as that the Queen had a cold in her head (one of Cheapside's nieces had a nest behind a shutter in Buckingham Palace); there was a dog show on at the Agricultural Hall; the Prime Minister had tripped over his own gown, going up the steps at the opening of Parliament, and fallen on his nose; a

ship had arrived at the East India Docks with
three real live pirates on board, captured in the
China Sea, etc. etc.

I could always tell when he had arrived at the
Doctor's house by the great commotion raised.
Gub-Gub or Jip the dog could be heard yelling in
the garden that the little Londoner had come.
And no matter how low our spirits were, Cheapside would not be in the house two minutes, chattering and twittering and giggling over his own
silly little Cockney jokes, before everybody would
be roaring with laughter or listening with great
attention to the news he had to tell. He always
brought us also the latest comic songs from the
city. Some of these that staid old housekeeper,
Dab-Dab, said were very vulgar; but I noticed she
often had much difficulty to keep from laughing
with the rest of us, nevertheless.

And then that very extraordinary character,
Matthew Mugg, the cats'-meat-man, was a comfort to me too. I did not leave the Doctor's place
much and there were days when I was lonely
for human company. At such times, now and
then, Matthew would drop in for a cup of tea, and
I was always glad to see him. We would sit and
chat over old times, about the Doctor and our
adventures, and make guesses as to what he
might be doing there, now, up in the Moon.

It was a good thing for me that I had plenty to
keep me busy, I suppose. Looking after ordinary
needs of the house, the garden and the animals
was not all I had to attend to. There were the
Doctor's instruments — microscopes and all sorts
of delicate scientific apparatus which he used in

his experiments; these I kept dusted and oiled and in apple-pie order.

Then there were his notes – shelves and shelves full of them. They were very valuable. John Dolittle himself had never been very orderly or careful about his notes, although he would not have had a single page of them lost for anything in the world. He had always said to me, 'Stubbins, if ever the house catches fire, remember, save the animals and the notes first and take care of the house afterwards.'

I therefore felt a great responsibility about those notes. Their safe-keeping was my first duty. And thinking about the possibility of fire I decided to move them away from the house altogether.

So I built a sort of underground library outside. With the help of Jip and Gub-Gub I dug out a place at the end of the garden, tunnelling into the side of a small hill near the old zoo.

It was a lovely spot. The wide lawn sloped gently up to a rise of about twenty feet, on the top of which a beautiful grove of weeping willows swept the grass with their graceful trailing branches. It was a part of the Doctor's big garden of which I was particularly fond. After we had burrowed out a big hole, the size of a large room, we took stones and timbers and built them into the sides to keep the earth from falling in. We floored it with some more stones; and after we had roofed it over, we covered the roof with earth two feet deep. A door was set on hinges in the front. Then we sowed grass all over the top and the sides, so it looked like the rest of the lawn.

'He always brought the latest comic songs from the city'

Nothing could be seen but the entrance. It was entirely fireproof.

Gub-Gub called it the *Underground Dolittle Library*, and he was very proud of having helped in the building of it. Not only that, but he was still more proud that his name was so often mentioned in those stacks and stacks of writing which we piled against the walls inside. On winter nights the animals often asked me to read aloud to them by the big kitchen fire, the same as the Doctor had done. And Gub-Gub always wanted me to read those parts from the books which spoke about him. He liked particularly to hear about himself and his great performances in the days of the Puddleby Pantomime. The other animals were not always pleased at this.

'Oh, gosh, Gub-Gub!' said Jip. 'I should think you'd get tired of hearing about yourself *all* the time.'

'But why?' said Gub-Gub. 'Am I not the most important pig in history?'

'Poof!' growled Jip in disgust. 'Most important pig on the garbage heap, you mean!'

But the day came when, as general manager of the Doctor's home, I found myself in difficulties. You cannot keep a family of animals and yourself on nothing at all. What money I had made shortly after my own return from the Moon was all used up. True, a good deal of food could be raised on the place. Wild ducks (friends of Dab-Dab's) brought us eggs. With the animals' help I kept the garden in very good condition. I pruned the apple trees as the Doctor had told me; and the kitchen garden was always well planted with vegetables.

Gub-Gub the pig was the one most interested in this. Although his habit of digging with his nose instead of a spade was somewhat untidy, he was a great help in keeping watch over everything as it grew. A pig was much better for this – in many ways – than a gardener. 'Tommy,' he would say, 'the cut-worms are getting at the celery roots.' Or, 'Tommy, the caterpillars are spoiling the cabbages – and the new spinach needs watering.'

Some of the vegetables I exchanged with neighbours, who had farms, for milk; and after I had learned how to make cheese from milk I could supply the white mouse with his favourite food.

But I needed money to buy a lot of other household things like candles, matches and soap. And some of the animals, although they were not meat-eaters, could not be fed from the garden. For instance, there was the old lame horse in the stable whom the Doctor had told me especially to look after. The hay and the oats in his stable were all gone. What grass he could eat from the lawns was already cropped down to the roots. He must have oats to keep his strength up. No, there was nothing for it; I must make some money, earn some money. But how?

# Chapter Two
## THE CATS'-MEAT-MAN'S ADVICE

I WENT out into the garden to think. I always seemed to be able to think better in that great garden of the Doctor's than anywhere else. I wandered down towards the new library and from there into the zoo. This quiet spot, enclosed by high walls on which the peach trees grew, had once been a very busy place. Here we had kept the Rat and Mouse Club, the Home for Cross-bred Dogs, and all the other institutions for animals' comfort and happiness. They were all deserted now, with nothing but a few early swallows skimming over the grass which the old lame horse had nibbled short and neat and trim.

I felt very sad. Nothing seemed the same without the Doctor. I began pacing to and fro, thinking about my problem. I heard the latch in the garden door click. I turned. There stood Matthew Mugg, the cats'-meat-man.

'Oh, hullo, Matthew!' I cried. 'I'm glad to see you.'

'My, Tommy!' said he. 'You do look serious. Anything the matter?'

'Yes, Matthew,' I said. 'I've got to get a job —

must make some money. Need it for
housekeeping.'

'Well, what kind of a job do you want?' he asked.

'Any kind, Matthew,' said I, 'any kind that I can
get.'

' 'Ave you been to your father about it? Why
can't you 'elp 'im in 'is business and earn money
that way?'

He started walking back and forth at my side.

'Yes, I've been to see my parents. But it wasn't
much use. Father's business is too small for him
to need an assistant — even if I were any good at
shoemaking, which I'm not.'

'Humph!' said the cats'-meat-man. 'Let me
think.'

'You see,' I said, 'it can't be a job which will take
me away from here. There is too much that I must
attend to — the garden and the rest. And besides,
there's the Doctor's return. I wouldn't be away
from here at the moment he gets home for
anything in the world. You haven't told any one
about our trip to the Moon, have you, Matthew?'

He tapped his pipe out against the heel of his
boot.

'Not a word, Tommy, not a word.'

'That's right, Matthew. It must be kept an
absolute secret. We have no idea what he will be
like to look at when he arrives. We don't want
journalists coming around and writing up
reports.'

'No,' said Matthew. 'That would bring the whole
world clattering at the gates. Everybody would
want to 'ave a look at the man from the Moon.'

'Quite so, Matthew; that's another reason why

I have to have a job. I don't know what the Doctor
may need when he gets here. He may be sick; he
may need special kinds of food. And I haven't a
penny in the house.'

'I know, I know,' said Matthew, shaking his
head. 'Money, money, money, what a curse it is!
– as the good man said himself. Can't seem to do
nothing without it though. But look 'ere, Tommy,
you shouldn't 'ave no trouble findin' a job. 'Cause
you got eddication, see?'

'Well, I've *some* education, Matthew. But what
good does it do me here in Puddleby? If I was able
to get away and go to London, now, that would be
different.'

'Oh, listen,' said the cats'-meat-man. 'You boys
all think you 'ave to go to London to make yer
fortunes – same as Dick Whittington. But young
men what 'as eddication can make a good livin'
'ere in Puddleby. You can read and write and do
'rithmetic. Why can't you be a clerk in the
Puddleby Bank, or a secketary, or somethin' like
that?'

'But, Matthew,' I cried, 'don't you see? I'd have
to stay at work in the town after it was dark –
in the winter months anyhow. And as you know
the Doctor told me to watch the Moon for signals
of his coming down. Of course it is true the
animals take their turns too, watching for the
smoke signals. But I would have to be there even
if I'm sleeping, so that I could be called at once
if – er – if –'

I don't exactly know why I broke off without
finishing what I had to say. But I suppose my
voice must have sounded uncertain, puzzled and

upset, because Matthew suddenly looked up from refilling his pipe and said, 'But, Tommy, you ain't worried, are yer? – I mean, about the Doctor's returnin'. You feel sure 'e *is* comin' back from the Moon?'

'Oh, yes,' I said. 'I suppose so.'

'*Suppose* so!' cried Matthew. 'Why, of course 'e will, Tommy! John Dolittle's one of them men what never comes to 'arm. 'E'll get back all right. Don't you worry.'

'But supposing the Moon Man won't let him come?' I said.

'It'll take a good deal more than a bloomin' Moon Man to stop John Dolittle from gettin' away if 'e wants to.'

'Well, but – er – Matthew,' I said, 'I sometimes wonder if he does *want to come back.*'

Matthew's eyebrows went up higher than ever.

'*Want* to come back!' he gasped. 'What d'yer mean?'

'Matthew Mugg,' I said, 'you know the Doctor cannot be judged the same as other folk. I mean, you never can tell what he'll do next. We found a very curious state of affairs in the Moon. It is a year now since he has been gone. I haven't said anything about it to the animals in the house here, but the last few weeks I've begun to wonder if John Dolittle has not perhaps decided to stay on the Moon – for good.'

'Oh, what an idea, Tommy!' said he. 'Why would 'e want to do that? From what you told me about the Moon, it didn't sound like a pleasant place at all.'

'It was not an unpleasant place, Matthew. It

was very strange and creepy at first. But when
you got used to it – no, you could not call it
unpleasant. Dreadfully lonely, but the most
peaceful place either the Doctor or I had ever
seen.'

'Well, but, Tommy, you don't mean to tell me
that a busy man like John Dolittle would throw
up all the things 'e's interested in 'ere on the
Earth and settle down on the Moon, just for the
sake of peace and quiet?'

'He might, Matthew,' I answered sadly. 'I've
often remembered, since I left him, something he
said when we first learned about the Moon
Council, from the whispering vines up there. "Our
world," he said, "down on the Earth is dog eat dog.
Fighting, fighting all the time. Here in the Moon
they manage things better. Life is arranged and
balanced. Even the plants and trees are not
allowed to crowd one another out. The birds,
instead of eating up the bees and insects, eat up
the extra seed of the plants and flowers so they
will not spread too fast." You see, Matthew, the
Great Council of Moon Life planned and watched
over everything so that peace reigned – in an
almost perfect world. You can understand how
such a state of things would appeal to a man like
John Dolittle. And there is nothing to stop him
from staying as long as he likes – if he thinks he's
doing more good up there than he can down here.
Now do you see?'

'Yes, but what I don't see is, 'ow 'e can be doing
any good up there.'

'Why, by looking after the Moon Man, Matthew.
The Doctor had often told me that Otho Bludge,

the only man in the Moon and the President of the
Life Council, was the greatest human being that
ever lived. He might be ignorant according to the
ideas of a country bumpkin or a nine-year-old
schoolboy down here – he could hardly be otherwise, born in the Stone Age as he was; but his was
the brain that worked out the Moon Council and
all that it did. And his was the hand that held it
together and kept it working. His great trouble,
as I've told you, was rheumatism. "Stubbins," the
Doctor said to me, "if anything ever happens to
Otho Bludge I fear it will be the end of the
Council. And the end of the Council must mean
that all this great work they have built up for
happy peaceful living will fall apart and crumble
away." '

Matthew frowned.

'Well, but still I can't imagine, Tommy,' said he,
'that the Doctor would chuck up all 'is connections
down 'ere just for the sake of plants and insects
and birds on the Moon. After all, this is the world
what 'e was born in.'

'Oh, I don't mean that he would forget us all
down here, thoughtlessly, or anything like that.
You know how utterly unselfish he is. If he thinks
it is necessary to act as doctor for the Moon Man,
he might stay on and on and on. He has for many
years now been dreadfully disappointed in human
beings and their stupid, unfair treatment of
animals. And another thing: we discovered that
life seemed to go on to tremendous lengths
up there. Some of the talking plants told us that
they were thousands of years old – the bees and
birds too. And the age of the Moon Man himself

is so great that not even the Doctor could calculate it.'

'Humph!' said Matthew thoughtfully. 'Strange place, the Moon.'

'I've sometimes wondered,' I added, 'if the Doctor had some ideas about everlasting life.'

'What do you mean, Tommy? Living for ever?'

'Yes, for the Moon Man – and perhaps for himself, for John Dolittle, as well. That vegetable diet, you know. A world where nobody, nothing dies! Maybe that's what he sees. If the Moon Man is wearing out a little now – but only after thousands of years – and the Doctor thinks it just requires the help of our science and medicine to keep him living indefinitely, I'm afraid, Matthew, terribly afraid, that he would be greatly tempted to stay.'

'Oh, come, come, Tommy,' said the cats'-meat-man. 'Meself, I think it's much more likely, if 'e 'as discovered the secret of everlastin' life, that 'e'll be wantin' to bring it down to old Mother Earth to try it on the folks 'ere. You mark my words, one of these fine nights 'e'll come tumblin' in on top of you, all full of mooney ideas what 'e wants to try out on the poor British public. You mark my words.'

'I hope you're right, Matthew,' I said.

'O' course I'm right, Tommy,' said he. 'We ain't seen the last of our old friend yet – not by a long chalk. And even if 'e 'asn't got no other 'umans to persuade 'im to come back, don't forget 'e 'as Polynesia, 'is parrot, and Chee-Chee the monkey with 'im. They're somethin' to be reckoned with. Why, that parrot, by 'erself, would talk down the whole House o' Lords in any argument! 'E'll come.'

'But it is a whole year, Matthew, that he's been gone.'

'Well, maybe 'e wanted to see what the spring and summer was like up there.'

'Yes, he did say something once about wishing to see the difference in the seasons on the Moon.'

'There you are!' Matthew spread out his hands in triumph. ' 'E's been gone a twelve-month — seen the spring, summer, autumn and winter on the Moon. You can expect 'im back anyday now, you mark my words. Cheer up, young man. Don't be down-'earted. Now let's get back to this job you was a' thinkin' of. You said you wanted some sort of a job what you could do at 'ome, didn't yer — so as you could keep one eye on the Moon like?'

'That's it, Matthew.'

'Humph!' grunted the cats'-meat-man. 'Now let me see. . . . Yes, I 'ave it! You remember that butcher what I buys my meat from to feed the cats and dogs with?'

'Oh, that round fat man with the little button of a nose?'

'Yes, that's 'im. Old Simpson. Now listen: Simpson couldn't never do figures, see? Always gettin' 'is books mixed up, sendin' wrong bills to people and 'avin' no end of rows with 'is customers. 'E's very sensitive about it. 'Is missus could do 'is figurin' for 'im but 'e won't let 'er, see? Doesn't like to admit that 'e can't add up straight. Now maybe I can persuade 'im to let me bring you

'is books twice a week; and you can put 'em right
and make out 'is bills proper for 'im, see?'

'Oh, Matthew,' I cried, 'that would be splendid
if you could!'

'Well, Tommy,' said he, 'I'll see what can be
done. I'll go and 'ave a chat with old Simpson in
the mornin', and I'll let you know. Now I got to
be off. Don't worry, Tommy, everything's goin' to
be all right.'

# Chapter Three
## CHEAPSIDE CALLS ON US

THE cats'-meat-man was quite successful. Obadiah Simpson, the butcher, was only too glad to hear of some one who would do his bookkeeping for him without telling anybody about it. Matthew Mugg brought me two large brandnew ledgers, as they were called, heavy, redbound, blank books with *OBADIAH SIMPSON & SONS – BUTCHERS: PUDDLEBY-ON-THE-MARSH* stamped in gold on their covers. With these, twice every week, he brought also an envelope full of greasy slips of paper on which were written the butcher's sales of meat to his customers.

The writing was awful and very hard to make out. Most of the customers' names were spelled wrong – often many different ways in one batch of bills. But after I had asked Matthew to get the proper spelling of the names for me I entered up each customer in the big elegant red books. I used a bold round handwriting, very elegant, I thought. It was in fact a boyish copy of Doctor Dolittle's. But anyhow, alongside of poor Simpson's dreadful-looking pothooks of letters and figures it did look very clear, grown-up and business-like.

The butcher was delighted with my work. I learned afterwards that he told his family that the book-keeping and the bold round handwriting were his own and that he had taken a special course in mathematics from a professor!

He paid me three shillings and sixpence a week. It does not sound much, I know. But in those days money went a great deal further than it does now. By economizing I was able to buy the things I needed for the house and the animals and I even managed to save a little out of it for a rainy day. And it was a good thing, too, that I did, as I will explain later on.

Spring was now turning into summer and the days were getting long again. One late afternoon we were sitting down to tea, and although daylight still lasted, a beautiful, pale full Moon hung in the sky. The animals were gathered around the table in the kitchen.

'Who is on duty watching the Moon tonight, Tommy?' asked Jip, looking up at the sky through the window.

'Too-Too,' I said. 'He will be there till midnight, then I will go up, Jip.'

'Listen, Tommy,' said the dog, 'I see some cloud banks over in the west there. What will happen if the clouds spread over the Moon just at the moment when the Doctor wants to set off the smoke signals?'

'You can see the Earth from the Moon just as plainly as you can see the Moon from here,' I said, 'only the Earth looks much larger. You remember

I told you the earthlight on the Moon was much stronger than the moonlight is on the Earth. If the Doctor sees clouds around the side of the Earth that is facing towards the Moon he will put off signalling till they clear away.'

'Yes, but suppose,' said Jip, 'that he is trying to get away secretly, without letting the Moon Man know; he might miss a chance that way which he would never get again.'

'I am afraid, Jip,' I answered, 'that getting off the Moon without Otho Bludge knowing it would be impossible for the Doctor – or anybody else.'

'It doesn't seem to me,' squeaked the white mouse, 'from what Tommy has told us about that horrid old Moon Man, that John Dolittle will stand any chance at all of leaving without his permission *and* his help. Isn't that so, Tommy?'

'Er – yes, I'm afraid it is, pretty much,' I answered. 'You see, gathering together enough of that special wood I told you about is a big job. To make a smoke explosion big enough to be seen from here you need to have a regular mountain of the stuff.'

'Is there any other way for him to get down,' asked Jip, 'except by using the giant moth who took you both up there?'

'Well, Jip,' I said, 'that's the only means that *I* know he could use. Still, you must remember, that I was only on the Moon for a short time. And although we went part way into the further side of the Moon – the side you never see from here – we had not explored it all when I left, by any means. The Doctor may have discovered new

animals since – flying insects and birds, you
know – which I never saw. He might get help
from them.'

'But look here,' said Gub-Gub, 'didn't you say
that all the creatures and plants on the Moon
obeyed the orders of Otho Bludge because he was
President of the Council? Well, how could they
help–'

'Oh, do be quiet!' snapped Dab-Dab. 'Enough of
your everlasting questions. The Doctor will get
down in his own time and his own way.'

I was glad of the old housekeeper's interruption.
For months now I had had to answer a never-end-
ing stream of enquiries about the Doctor and his
chances of getting off the Moon. With her clever
motherly sense, Dab-Dab had seen that my heart
was sinking lower and lower as the months went
by, while I still tried to keep up a cheerful front.
Yet no one was more uneasy about the Doctor's
safety – though she did not show it – than Dab-
Dab herself. I had found her more than once of
late secretly dusting his room, brushing his
clothes and putting his shaving things in order
with tears in her eyes. She confessed to me, years
afterwards, that she had given up all hope of seeing her dear old friend again when the tenth
month had passed.

'Yes, but what I don't understand,' said the
white mouse, 'is how the–'

'There are a lot of things you don't understand,' Dab-Dab put in. 'Who wants a piece of hot
toast?'

'I do,' said Gub-Gub.

I took a large plate full of toast from the hearth

and set it on the table. And for a while we all
munched away and drank tea in silence.

'What are you thinking about, Gub-Gub?' asked
the white mouse presently.

'I was thinking of the kitchen garden of Eden
— if you must know,' grunted Gub-Gub with his
mouth full.

'The *kitchen* garden of Eden! Tee, hee, hee!'
tittered the white mouse. 'What an idea!'

'Well, they had apples in the garden of Eden,
didn't they?' said Gub-Gub. 'And if they had
orchards they must have had a kitchen garden. I
do wish the Bible had said more about it. I could
have used it very nicely in my Encyclopedia of
Food.'

'What would have you called it?' tittered the
white mouse. ' "Chapter on Biblical Eating"?'

'I don't know,' said Gub-Gub seriously. 'But
listen: I did know a biblical family once.'

'You did!' cried the white mouse. 'A biblical
family!'

'Certainly,' said Gub-Gub. 'Very biblical. They
all wore bibs — the children, the parents, and
even the grandfather. But I do wish I knew what
Adam and Eve ate besides apples.'

'Oh, well, why bother?' sighed Jip. 'Just make
it up out of your fat head as you go along. Who
will know the difference? Nobody was ever there.'

'Why not call it "Heavenly Vegetables"?' said
the white mouse, carefully brushing the toast
crumbs out of his silky whiskers.

'Yes, I was thinking of that,' said Gub-Gub.
'After all, what would heaven be without
vegetables?'

' "Well, they had apples in the garden of Eden, didn't they?"
said Gub-Gub'

'Just heaven,' said Jip with a sigh.

'Sh!' said Dab-Dab. 'What's that noise?'

'Why, it's Cheapside! Look!' cried the white mouse. 'At the window.'

We all glanced up and there, sure enough, was the Cockney sparrow tapping on the glass with his stubby bill. I ran and pushed the window up. He hopped inside.

'What ho, me 'earties!' he chirped. ' 'Ere we are again! The old firm – what, 'avin' tea? Good, I'm just in time. I always makes an 'abit of arrivin' places just in time for tea.'

He flew on to the table and began helping me to eat my piece of toast.

'Well,' said he, 'what's new in Puddleby?'

'Nothing much, Cheapside,' I said. 'I have a small job which brings in a little money – enough to keep us going. But we always expect *you* to bring the news, you know. How is Becky?'

'Oh, the wife,' said he. 'She's all right. Yer know the old sayin', "naught can never come to 'arm." Ha, ha! We're busy buildin' the new spring nest now – yes, same old place, St Edmund's left ear, south side of the Cathedral. But we got a new architect in charge of St Paul's now. And what d'yer think was the first thing 'e did? Why, 'e gave orders to 'ave all the saints *washed*! It's a fact. Sacrilegious, I calls it. And ain't we sparrows got no rights neither? Mussin' up our nests with dirty water! Why, me and Becky 'ave built our nest in St Edmund's left ear for six years now. Thought we was goin' to 'ave to move over to the Bank of England *this* spring – straight, we did. But at last them bloomin' masons got finished with their

old moppin' and sloppin' and we're back at the old
address for another year. Any word of the Doctor?'

A little silence fell over us all.

'No, Cheapside,' I said at last. 'No signals as yet.
But tell me, what is the news from London?'

'Well,' said Cheapside, 'they're all talkin' about
this 'ere eclipse of the Moon.'

'What are *clips of the Moon*?' asked Gub-Gub.

'An eclipse, Gub-Gub,' I said, 'is when the Earth
gets between the Sun and the Moon — exactly in
between. The Earth's shadow is then thrown upon
the Moon and its light is put out — for us. When
is this eclipse, Cheapside?'

'It's tonight, Tommy,' said the sparrow. 'It's the
first full eclipse in I don't know how many years.
And everybody up in London is getting out their
telescopes and opery-glasses so as to be ready to
see it. That's why I come 'ere tonight. "Becky," I
says to the missus, "I believe I'll take a run down
to Puddleby this evenin'." "What d'yer want to do
that for?" she says. "What about the nest
buildin'?" she says. "Ain't you interested in yer
children no more?" "Ho no!" I says to 'er, I says.
"It ain't that, old girl. But when a feller's 'ad as
many families as I've 'ad, yer can't expect — well,
the newness of the idea gets worn off a bit, you
know. There's an eclipse tonight, Becky," I says,
"and this 'ere city air is so foggy. I'd like to run
down to the Doctor's place and see it from the
country. You can finish the nest by yerself. It's
nearly done already." "Oh, very well," she says.
"You and your eclipses! It's a fine father you are!
Run along." And 'ere I am, the old firm. Let's 'ave
another piece of toast, Dab-Dab.'

'Do you know what time the eclipse is supposed to be, Cheapside?' I asked.

'A few minutes after eleven o'clock, Tommy,' said he. 'I'm going to go up and watch it from the roof, I am.'

# Chapter Four
## THE ECLIPSE OF THE MOON

AT Cheapside's words a great chattering broke out among the animals. Every one of them decided he wanted to stay up and see the eclipse. Usually our household was a very free one, quite different in that way – as well as many others – from a household of people. Everybody went to bed at whatever hour he wished – though if we did not want a scolding from Dab-Dab we all had to be pretty much on time for meals. The last few months, however (even while we carefully took turns watching the Moon for the smoke signals), we had been going to bed pretty early in order to save candles.

Gub-Gub was dreadfully afraid that he would miss the eclipse by falling asleep. This was something he did very easily at any hour at all. He made us promise to wake him if he should doze off before eleven o'clock. Cheapside's coming had cheered us all up. We certainly needed it. I thought something should be done to celebrate.

And so, as it turned out, that particular eclipse of the Moon was made a very special occasion and a sort of a party.

Immediately after tea I ran down to the town
and spent a little of the money I had saved up on
some things for a special supper. I got the right
time, too, while I was shopping and corrected the
grandfather's clock in the hall when I got back to
the house.

We had a very happy meal, everybody chattering and laughing over the sparrow's ridiculous
jokes and songs. As usual, I was asked no end of
questions – this time about eclipses and what
they were like. I found some of them very difficult
to answer, because, though I had seen an eclipse
of the Sun once, I had never seen one of the Moon.

All the animals wanted to make sure of a good
place to watch from, where they could see the
show properly. This was not easy. There were
several high trees near the house; and at half-past
ten the Moon looked as though it might very soon
be hidden by their top branches – that is, if one
tried to watch the eclipse from the garden. So
Gub-Gub said he wanted to see it from the roof,
the same as Cheapside. I explained to him that it
was easy for the birds, like Too-Too, Dab-Dab and
the sparrow – and even for the white mouse,
because they could cling to the ridge and keep
their balance, but that it would be much more
difficult for him and Jip and myself.

However, there was a trap-door in the roof
which let you out from the attic on to the tiles,
close to the big chimney. In the attic I managed
to rig up two step-ladders with a sort of platform,
made out of boards and packing-cases on the top.
By standing on this we were able to stick our
heads out of the trap-door.

It was a fine place for a view. I could see the town of Puddleby, three miles away, even the buildings and everything – the church tower, the town hall, the winding river, all bathed in the light of the Moon.

On the platform Jip, Gub-Gub and I stationed ourselves to wait. The white mouse I had brought up in my pocket. I let him go on the tiles where, with squeals of joy, he ran along the ridge or capered up and down the steep slopes of the roof, absolutely fearless, just as though he were on solid ground.

'Can't I get out on to the tiles too, Tommy?' asked Gub-Gub. 'Whitey is going to get a much better view than we can here – with just our noses poking out of this hole.'

'No,' I said, 'better not. You can see the Moon quite well from where you are. Whitey can cling on to steep places where none of us could.'

However, while my back was turned, Gub-Gub did scramble out on to the roof – with sad consequences. I heard a terrible squawk and turning around I saw him lose his balance and go rolling down the slope of the roof like a ball.

'Great Heavens!' I said to Jip. 'He'll be killed – or badly hurt anyway.'

'Don't worry,' said Jip. 'He's well padded. Most likely he'll just bounce when he hits the ground. You can't hurt that pig.'

With a dreadful shriek Gub-Gub disappeared into the darkness over the edge of the slope and for a second we listened in silence. But instead of the thud of his falling on the garden path, the sound of a big splash came up to us. The white mouse

ran down the slope and looked over the edge of the
rain-gutter.

'It's all right, Tommy,' he called back to me.
'He's fallen into the rain-water barrel.'

I jumped to the attic floor, ran down the stairs
and out into the garden.

In those days all country houses had rain-water
barrels. They were big and set close to the walls
to catch rain-water from the roof. Into one of these
poor Gub-Gub had fallen – luckily for him. When
I came up he was swimming and gasping in the
water, quite unable to get out, but not hurt in the
least. I fished him up to the top, carried him into
the kitchen and rubbed him with a towel. He was
a wetter but a wiser pig.

When I had got him dry I heard the hall clock
strike eleven and we hurried back to the trap-door.

As we started to get up on to the platform
Jip called to me, 'Hurry, Tommy, hurry! It's
beginning!"

Then I heard Too-Too calling from the other end
of the roof, 'Here it is. The shadow! Look! The
shadow creeping over the Moon.'

I sprang out of the trap-door and stood on the
ridge, steadying myself with one hand on the
chimney.

It was indeed a remarkable sight. There was not
a cloud in the sky. A great round shadow, like a
tea-tray, was creeping slowly across the face of
the Moon. The country about us had been all
flooded with light, almost like day. But now the
world slowly began to darken as the Moon's light
went out, shut off by the giant shadow of the
Earth. Even Puddleby River, which had shone so

clearly, was gone in the darkness. Little by little the shadow crept on until the Moon was hidden altogether; only a faint, pale, glowing ring – like a will-o'-the-wisp – was left standing in the sky where it had been. It was the blackest night.

'My goodness, Tommy!' whispered Gub-Gub, 'isn't it exciting? Will it stay this way?'

'Not for long, Gub-Gub,' I said. 'In a few seconds you will see the Moon again, just the edge of it at first, when our shadow passes off it.'

'But I don't see myself there,' said Gub-Gub. 'We're sitting up on top of the house, as plain as a pikestaff. There ought to be the shadow of a pig and a dog and a boy there.'

'Tee, hee, hee!' tittered the white mouse out of the darkness at my elbow.

'No, Gub-Gub,' I said. 'Our bodies can throw a shadow on the ground, or a wall, both by sunlight and moonlight. But we are too small – as far away from it as this – to throw a shadow on the Moon.'

'Humph! I'm very disappointed,' grunted Gub-Gub. 'I would have liked to see my shadow on the Moon.'

'You are a kind of a comical scientist, you are, piggy,' chirped Cheapside from the chimney top above our heads. 'An eclipse of the bacon, ha!'

'But, listen, Tommy,' said Jip. 'You said the Moon's light is only the light of the Sun reflected back to us here, the same as a mirror, didn't you? Very well then: if the Earth on which we stand is now in between the Sun and the Moon – throwing a shadow over it – then any one in the moon

at this moment will have the light of the Sun cut
off, wouldn't he?'

'Yes, Jip,' I said. 'That's quite right. The Moon
is now having an eclipse of the Sun while we are
having an eclipse of the Moon. . . . There you are,
Gub-Gub, the shadow is passing off now. You can
just see a thin line of the Moon beginning to show
on the − my goodness, what was that?'

'Tommy! Tommy!' screamed Dab-Dab. 'Did you
see that? A puff of smoke − just at the end of the
white line of the Moon!'

'Yes, I saw it!' I shouted back. 'Yes, look − there
it goes again!'

'White smoke!' said Jip solemnly.

'The signal, the signal at last!' cried Too-Too.

'It's the Doctor!' said the white mouse.

'Yes, it's the Doctor, all right,' chirped Cheapside. ' 'E's comin' back to us. Gawd bless 'im!'

# Chapter Five
## I SEND FOR HELP

THE Doctor's little house on the Oxenthorpe Road had in its time seen many days and nights of excitement and thrill. But I don't believe that it ever saw anything quite as uproarious and crazy as it did now. All the animals asked me a question at once, and, without waiting for an answer, asked me another. When they were not asking questions they were chattering and cheering or giving advice, or just singing for sheer joy. And I must admit I was pretty well excited myself.

'Cheapside,' I said, 'fly over to Matthew Mugg's house, will you? He'll be in bed, but tap on his window and wake him up. Point to the Moon. He'll understand. Get him to come here right away. Bring him in his nightshirt if necessary, but get him here. I may need his help.'

'Okay!' chirped the sparrow, and with a flirt of his wings he was under way.

'How long do you think it will be before the Doctor gets here?' asked Gub-Gub. 'What will he do if a storm comes up? Will he be hungry? Yes, of course he will. I'll go and dig up some of the spring onions at once.'

'Listen, Tommy,' said the white mouse. 'What
will he be wearing? Most likely his clothes will
be all in rags after this long time, won't they?
I'll go and thread some needles for him right
away.'

Dab-Dab was a changed duck. Instead of carrying her usual look of seriousness, care, and
responsibility, she was now weeping and smiling
at the same time.

'Just to think of it!' she kept muttering. 'The
dear man! On his way back at last! Which room
shall we put him in, Tommy — his old one? It's
the only large bedroom, facing east — and he
always did like to wake up with the morning sun
on the windows, you know. You've got it full of
dried plants and specimens. But no matter, we'll
soon clear it. I'll go and make his bed up.'

'There is no hurry about that, Dab-Dab,' I said.
'He can't get down to the Earth for many hours
yet.'

The eclipse was nearly over now. We waited a
few minutes — just to make sure we did not miss
any further signals. Then, after the shadow had
cleared away entirely and the Moon sailed the
sky again in all her glory, we went down into the
house.

'Listen, everybody,' I said when we were
gathered in the kitchen: 'you know we agreed to
keep the Doctor's visit to the Moon a secret. And
we have. That is one of the reasons why I have
hardly left the house since I came back to you —
I did not want to be asked questions by people I
might meet. Now it is more important than ever
that we say nothing — nothing to any living

thing, you understand — of John Dolittle's return.
Do not speak of it even to your animal friends or
we shall have a string of cows and dogs and horses
a mile long waiting at the gate to greet him. That
will attract the attention of people and the Doctor
will get no peace day or night. He may be very
much in need of rest and sleep when he arrives.
So remember: not a word.'

'Tommy,' Jip whispered, 'you're not fearing he'll
be sick when he gets here, are you?'

'I'm not fearing anything, Jip,' I answered. 'But
on the other hand I don't know what to expect.
The journey down here is a very trying and hard
one, as I told you. The changes of air and gravity
and climate are awfully sudden and disturbing.
John Dolittle has been more than a year on the
moon. I was only up there a short time. It may be
much more difficult for him to get used to the
Earth again than it was for me. I would feel
happier if I had another doctor here in case he
needs medical care. But Matthew will be along
presently. I'll be able to send him into the town
if we need anything.'

'But everything will be all shut up now,
Tommy,' said he. 'It's nearly midnight.'

'I doubt if we shall see the Doctor before tomorrow night, Jip,' I said. 'Even at the tremendous
speed that the giant moth travels, it takes a long
time. Then again he may not leave immediately
after signalling. He may wait a while. I have an
idea he chose the time of the eclipse for some
special reason. Too-Too, would you please see how
much money I have?'

'Yes, Tommy,' said the owl, 'right away.'

In those days we only had metal money, copper, silver and gold, except for large amounts. What I had saved I kept in the same old money-box the Doctor used. It stood in the same place, too — on the dresser shelf in the kitchen. Too-Too, who had always been a wizard at mathematics, now emptied the money-box into a flat dish and began to count up the coins.

'If he arrives in the daylight,' said Jip, 'what shall we do then? — I mean about people seeing him land. How are we going to keep it a secret?'

'I imagine the Doctor will think of that himself,' I said. 'Most likely he will time his departure from the Moon so as to land here in the dark. I think, Jip, we had better arrange for some one to stay on watch at the trap-door till the Moon sets. Will you go?'

'Certainly,' said Jip, and he made for the stairs.

'Tommy,' called Too-Too from the dresser, 'you have here exactly seven shillings and fourpence ha'penny. Let's see: you've had your job five weeks now. That means you've saved eighteen pence a week. Not bad, Tommy, not bad.'

'No,' I said; 'I didn't think I had so much. Well, we'll need it — and maybe a good deal more.'

There came a familiar *tap-tap* at the window-pane.

'Cheapside!' said the white mouse.

I let him in.

'You didn't take long,' I said. 'Did you find Matthew?'

'Yes,' said the sparrow. ' 'E's comin' right along

be'ind me. I can fly much quicker, see? So I come on ahead.'

It was not many minutes after Cheapside's return that Gub-Gub came in from the kitchen garden. He had a beautiful bunch of spring onions which he had gathered.

'I do love digging up onions by moonlight,' said he. 'There's something so poetic about it. Listen, Tommy, I saw Matthew's figure from the gate, way down the road, coming here on the run.'

At that moment Matthew burst into the room.

'Tommy!' he cried, all out of breath. 'You don't mean to say you got the signal!'

'That's it, Matthew,' I said. 'We all saw it – twice – two distinct puffs of smoke. Isn't it grand?'

'Why, I should say it is!' said the cats'-meat-man, sinking into a chair. 'I run all the way 'ere. Ain't done such a thing since I was a boy. I *thought* it was Cheapside, but then I couldn't be sure, because all sparrers look alike to me. Me and Theodosia 'ad gone to bed; but that blinkin' little bird woke us up – kept peckin' at the glass and pointin' to the Moon. My, I wish I could talk these bird languages, the same as you can! But at last I tumbled to the idea and I jumps into me clothes like a fireman and 'ere I am. 'Ow soon do yer expect the Doctor?'

'I can't tell, Matthew. My guess is some time tomorrow night. But I wanted to have you here right away to help me if necessary. You don't mind, do you?'

'I'm *dee*lighted, Tommy, *dee*lighted! I wouldn't

' "You don't mean to say you got the signal!" '

miss being 'ere to welcome the Doctor, not for nothin' in the world.'

All the animals were far too excited to go to bed that night. They kept skipping in and out of the house, peering at the Moon. Matthew Mugg sat up with me in the kitchen, where we talked till the dawn showed in the east windows.

# Chapter Six
## THE SOUND IN THE SKY

**E**VEN then, when daylight came, the cats'-meat-man and I only took short sleeps in our chairs, setting Too-Too on watch with orders to rouse us if anything happened.

About noon Dab-Dab woke us and said breakfast was ready. We were hungry and ate a hearty meal.

'We ought to get some things in from the town, Tommy,' said the housekeeper as she waited on us. 'The larder is pretty low in provisions.'

'All right, Dab-Dab,' I said. 'Tell me what you need.'

'I'm short of milk,' she said. 'The Doctor always drank a lot of milk. And I'm low on sugar, too. And – let me see – yes, tapioca, macaroni and three loaves of bread. I think that's all.'

I made out a list, gave it to Matthew with some money, and asked him to do the shopping for us. The cats'-meat-man was very proud of being a friend of John Dolittle's, so, fearing he might be tempted to talk, I reminded him once more as he set out for Puddleby to keep a closed mouth about the great event we were waiting for.

'Don't you worry, Tommy,' he said. 'I won't talk. But listen, would you mind if I was to tell my wife Theodosia? She was at me last night to tell 'er why I was rushin' off in such an 'urry. She always thinks I'm goin' poachin' when I stays out nights. But she knows 'ow to keep a secret. And, while Dab-Dab is a pretty good cook and housekeeper, we might be glad of 'er 'elp when the Doctor arrives. Theodosia would be right pleased to do anything she can for John Dolittle. And, yer know, women – they do know 'ow to make a place 'omelike for a welcome. They 'ave ideas – and good ones, too.'

'Why – er, yes, Matthew,' I said. 'I see no reason why you shouldn't tell Mrs Mugg.'

Not long after the cats'-meat-man had gone, the old lame horse came round to the kitchen door.

'Tommy,' said he, 'I see the woodshed is nearly empty. Maybe the Doctor will need a fire when he gets down. The nights are still pretty cool. Don't you think we ought to go and gather some wood?'

'Yes,' I said. 'I think we should. But how is your hoof?'

'Oh,' said he, 'not too bad. I have to limp a bit. But if you put those two wood baskets on my back I can manage them easy.'

So I got an axe and we went off into the small forest that bordered the Doctor's garden at the bottom. Here I chopped enough wood for three or four good fires. I loaded it into the baskets and the old horse carried it up to the shed.

It was about half-past four in the afternoon

when Matthew got back. Besides the stores I had sent him for, he brought Theodosia Mugg, his wife. I was glad to see her big motherly figure coming up the garden path. She was a very clever and capable woman, was Theodosia. This she had shown when she travelled with the Doctor in the circus, years ago, and had acted as wardrobe-woman in the famous Canary Opera which John Dolittle had put on in London.

Dab-Dab did not quite care for the idea of having any one share her duties as housekeeper. But she had always liked Theodosia, and very soon she saw that the good woman could get a lot more done in one hour than a duck could in three.

A few minutes after she arrived Mrs Mugg had all the carpets out on the lawn to be beaten; she had the lace curtains in the wash-tub to be cleaned; the kitchen floor was scrubbed; every dish in the house was spick and span. You never saw a house change so quickly.

'Oh, Master Tommy,' said she (I could never understand why I was just plain 'Tommy' to Matthew, but always 'Master Tommy' to his wife), 'ain't it wonderful to think of the Doctor's comin' back? It threw me all of a twitter — the news did, when Matthew told me — oh, would yer mind chasin' that pig out into the garden? 'E's muddin' up the clean floor.'

Gub-Gub, much to his disgust, was asked to leave.

'Yes,' she went on, 'Matthew told me too what you said about keepin' the Doctor's comin' a secret. Never fear, I don't want to be laughed at. People wouldn't believe you — not if you told 'em one quarter of what's true about the Doctor. Why, when I was workin' with 'im in the circus and 'e put on the Canary Opera, it was plain to every one in London that 'e could talk the languages of all them birds – just as if 'e come of a canary family 'isself. But even then, with it right under their noses, would people believe it? No. "Talk canary language!" says they. "Impossible! It's just trainin' tricks –" No, you needn't think I'd speak to any one about the Doctor's bein' in the Moon. I don't want to be laughed at. That's the way folks are: tell 'em anything new and they think you're cracked.'

Theodosia shook her head sadly and went on dusting the pantry cupboard.

'Yes,' I said. 'And I fancy that is partly why John Dolittle has kept so much to himself of late years. For one thing, many of the scientific discoveries he has made in natural history are far too extraordinary for people to believe; and for another, he does not want to be bothered with people fussing at him and admiring him and hindering him from working. Why, Jip told me that while he was running the opera in London it took him an hour of each day to sign the autograph albums that were sent for him for his signature.'

'It was worse than that, Master Tommy,' said Theodosia, 'sometimes. Indeed, we 'ad to get the 'elp of the police to keep the crowds away when they discovered what 'ouse 'e was livin' in in London – well, now look 'ere! This won't do. I mustn't stand gossipin'. I want to get this 'ouse finished before 'e comes.'

It began to get dark about a quarter-past seven. By that time the animals had all had sleep of some sort, even if it was only a few minutes. They now began to fuss around again, chatting in the garden in twos and threes, determined not to be caught napping at the last moment. I noticed some blackbirds and robins watching this moonlight garden party from the trees. So I sent out Dab-Dab to call the animals in.

When the Moon rose at a quarter-past eight, Matthew and I stationed ourselves at one of the bedroom windows. We left this window open.

'You feel sure 'e'll come tonight, Tommy, don't you?' asked the cats'-meat-man.

'Pretty certain, Matthew,' I said. 'I only hope he arrives in darkness. That's the one thing I'm afraid about now.'

'Well, the Doctor don't often go wrong on calculations,' said he.

'No,' I said, 'that's very true. But you see I'm by no means certain he'll come on the moth. If he does, he could be sure of his timing, because on our way up his watch never stopped. After we'd landed it went all wrong, on account of the gravity and different climate. But he noted down the exact number of hours it took us to get up there. However, Jamara Bumblelily was the only specimen of the giant moth we saw in the Moon. It is possible she may not be able to bring the Doctor on this trip.'

'What will 'e do, then?'

'I've no idea, Matthew,' I said. 'Perhaps he'll come on some other insect – which may take a longer or may take a shorter time.'

At that moment there was a scratching on the door.

'Tommy, Tommy!' called Jip through the door. 'Too-Too says he hears something – in the sky, a long way off. Listen and see if you can catch it!'

# Chapter Seven
## THE GREAT LOCUST

**B**OTH Matthew and I put our heads out of the window.

'Do you hear anything?' I asked.

'Not a thing, Tommy,' said the cats'-meat-man.

'Humph!' I said. 'Neither do I. But that's not surprising. That owl Too-Too can hear things that no human ear can ever catch. Why, once when we were—'

'Sh! – Listen!' whispered Matthew. 'Do you get that? A low humming noise.'

Then came another knocking on the door. This time it was Dab-Dab.

'Tommy,' she called. 'Come out into the garden – the back garden – quick!'

Matthew and I dashed for the door and down the stairs.

Behind the house, on the big lawn, we found all the animals with Theodosia, gazing skywards. And now I heard it: a deep, soft, purring kind of noise, still a long, long way off.

'Well, if that's a moth,' said Matthew, 'it's as big as a young town.'

'It isn't the moth,' I said. 'Jamara Bumblelily

made an entirely different sound. The Doctor's coming down on something else. We must get the lawn clear. Let's run that wheelbarrow into the shed, Matthew.'

'All right. I'll do it,' said the cats'-meat-man.

This fine sweep of turf had always been known as the Long Lawn. It was one part of that grand old garden of which the Doctor was very proud. Bordered by great elm trees on one side and by a long tall yew-hedge on the other, it ran in one unbroken sweep of a hundred and fifty yards, from the house at one end towards the fish-pond and the zoo at the other. At the bottom there was an old card house, a pavilion made like a small Greek temple out of gleaming white stone. On this lawn, the history of the place told us, a duel had been fought by merry gentlemen in brocade and lace ruffles, after they had quarrelled over their card game in the pavilion.

It was a romantic spot. And just to look at it by moonlight carried you back hundreds of years. I could not help wondering as I gazed upon it now whether, with all its memories of the past, it had ever seen anything as strange as it would see tonight.

It is curious that from the time when the hum in the sky could be first plainly heard, none of us spoke. We had all drawn away, close to the house, so as to leave the Long Lawn clear for the Doctor's landing. Silent, Matthew presently joined us. And there we all stood, faces upturned towards the Moon, too breathless with excitement to speak, while the booming drone of great wings grew louder and louder.

How long we waited I cannot tell. It may have been a minute, it may have been an hour. I know I had intended to note down the exact time the Doctor landed. He had so often reminded me of the importance, in keeping scientific or natural history notes, of putting down the date and the time of day. For this reason I had brought out with me one of his old watches which I had carefully set by the grandfather's clock in the hall. But I forgot to look at it. I forgot everything. All I thought of was that he was there – somewhere in the sky, with that tremendous growing sound – coming, coming back to us at last!

But though I lost all count of time that night, everything that actually happened I remember as sharply now as though it were drawn in pictures before my eyes at this moment. Somewhere in that space of time while we stood gazing, a great shadow swept suddenly between us and the Moon. For a little while it stood, hovering and humming, high up above the lawn. I could not yet make out much as to its shape. Then, like some roaring machine turned off sharply, the noise ceased. The air rested in a big dead silence.

I guessed that whatever creature it might be, it was probably now sailing with outspread wings, looking for a place to land. Next the shadow passed from off the smooth grass. Was it circling – circling downwards? Yes, because once more its great body shut off the light like a cloud.

And at last – *whish!* – it came skimming over the tree-tops in plain view. The air whistled like a fierce gust of wind as it banked around in a graceful curve and dropped on the turf before us.

*It filled the whole of the Long Lawn!*

It was clear to me now that it was some member of the grasshopper family. (Later I learned that it was a locust.) But for the present I was not so concerned with the nature of the insect as I was with what it carried.

Alone, I moved out into the moonlight towards it. On tiptoe, trying to see the top of its back, I peered upward. But the highest part of it was hidden by the curve of the body. The great locust, apparently exhausted by the long journey, lay absolutely still. Nothing moved anywhere.

A terrible fear came over me. Where was the Doctor? Had the hard journey proved too much for him? Or could it be that he had not come at all? Perhaps this great thing from the Moon's animal kingdom had only brought a message to us – maybe a message to say that John Dolittle had decided to stay on that other world after all.

Frantic at the thought, I started to scramble up the locust's wings, which were now folded at his sides. Beautiful, transparent wings they were, smooth and opal-coloured – with great hard veins running through them, standing out from the glassy surface like gnarled roots.

But suddenly I heard a voice, a harsh, grating, but well-remembered, well-loved voice. A parrot's! 'Chee-Chee, Chee-Chee! Wake up! We're here – in Puddleby. Shiver my timbers! You're not as sick as you think you are. Wake up!'

And then for the first time the Earth spoke back to the people from the Moon.

'Polynesia!' I shouted. 'Is that you? Where is the Doctor? Is he with you?'

'Yes, he's here all right,' called the parrot. 'But he's unconscious still. We've got to go easy with him. Had an awful time getting through the dead belt. Gosh, what a journey! I wonder if I can fly straight any more in this gravity? Look out! I'm coming down.'

I saw something shoot out off the top of the locust's back. It looked like a bundle of rags, turning over and over in the air. Then it landed on the grass at my feet with a distinct thud. Polynesia, ruffled and disgruntled, broke out into a long string of Swedish swear-words.

'Ouch!' she ended. 'Did you see that? Landed right on my nose, like a pudding! I've got to learn to fly all over again – at my time of life! All unbalanced and fluffed up! Just because that stupid old Moon doesn't keep the right kind of air. You haven't got a biscuit in your pocket, I suppose? I'm as hungry as a bear.'

I called to Dab-Dab to go and fetch me some from the pantry.

'But, Polynesia,' I said, 'what about the Doctor? You say he's unconscious?'

'Yes,' she said, 'but he's all right. Difficulty with his breathing, you know. Leave him to rest a little while. We'll get him down presently. Poor old Chee-Chee's seasick, or airsick, or whatever it is. The last few hours of the trip I was the only one on deck, the only one left to guide that blessed grasshopper to the garden here. That comes of my years of seafaring, Tommy. Hard as nails, hard as nails! So would you be if you had lived a hundred

'Like a bundle of rags, turning over and over'

and eighty years on sunflower seeds and biscuit
crumbs! Trouble with humans is they eat too
many different kinds of foods. Parrots have more
sense!'

She strutted a few paces with her funny, strad-
dling, sailor-like gait. Then she fell down on her
side.

'Drat it!' she muttered. 'This air is heavy! Can't
even walk straight.'

'But listen,' I said. 'The Doctor – can't we –'

'Sh!' she whispered. 'He's woken up. Look!'

I glanced towards the locust's back. An enormous foot was sliding down towards us. It was
followed by a still more enormous leg. Finally the
body came in sight. Polynesia and I moved back
a little. Then, with a run, the whole mass of an
unbelievably big human figure came slithering
down the locust's wings and slumped into a heap
on the lawn.

I rushed forward and gazed into the motionless
face. The eyes were closed. The skin was tanned
to a deep brown colour by sun and wind. But, for
me, there was no mistaking the mouth, the nose,
the chin.

It was John Dolittle.

# Chapter Eight
## THE DOCTOR'S VOICE

I RAN into the house for the brandy flask which was always kept in the dispensary. But when I got back the Doctor was standing up. He was eighteen feet three and a half inches high. (This I am sure of, because I measured him the next day while he was lying asleep.)

It is difficult to describe his appearance. His sun hat was home-made out of materials he had evidently gathered in the Moon and so were his clothes – all but his trousers. These were fashioned out of the blankets we had taken up with us.

'Doctor, Doctor!' I cried. 'Oh, I'm so glad to see you back!'

To my surprise he did not answer at once.

I noticed that Chee-Chee the monkey had got over his sickness enough to come down into one of the willows nearby, where Polynesia had joined him. Dab-Dab also had come forward and was now gazing at the Doctor with an odd expression, a mixture of motherly affection, worry, great joy and a little fear. But no one uttered a word. We

were all waiting in silence for this strange figure
before us to speak.

Presently the Doctor stretched down his hand
and took a couple of tottering, unsteady steps
towards me. He seemed dreadfully weak and sort
of dazed. Once he lifted up his left hand and
brushed it across his eyes, as though his sight, as
well as his legs, was uncertain. Then his enormous right hand grasped mine so that it disappeared entirely.

At last in a curious hesitating way he said:

'Why – why, it's Stubbins! Good old . . . good
old . . . S-s-s-stubbins. Er – er – how are you?'

The voice was the only part of him that had not
changed. If his face had been blue and he had
grown horns in the Moon no one, in any doubt
before, could be uncertain now of who it was that
spoke. That voice did something to his friends
over by the house, who still waited with almost
bated breath. For suddenly all of them, Jip, Gub-
Gub, the white mouse, Cheapside, Too-Too,
Matthew and Theodosia, broke out into resound-
ing cheers and came flocking across the lawn on
the run.

They formed a ring around him, all talking at
once.

He smiled and tried to say something to each of
them. But in a moment he stopped short,
swaying.

'Stubbins,' he muttered. 'I must sit down.'

He sank heavily to the grass and propped his
back against a tree.

'Can I get you anything, Doctor,' I asked.
'Brandy?'

'No, I'll be – be all right soon, Stubbins. It's my – er – er – breathing, you know. Funny how I've forgotten the language – partly. Haven't talked it in so long. Have to – er – stop to remember words.'

'Well, don't try to talk now, Doctor,' I said. 'Just rest here.'

'The change of air-pressure . . . c-c-catches my breath,' he murmured, closing his eyes. 'And the stronger gravity – with my weight. Never dreamed the change would be so great. Just take my pulse, will you?'

I took out the watch and held his wrist.

'It's all right, Doctor,' I said after a while. 'It's a little fast, but strong and regular.'

I turned to Theodosia and asked her to get some mattresses and bedding from the house. She was not sure where to look for them, so I went with her.

'Mercy, Master Tommy!' she whispered when we were inside. 'The Lord be praised 'e's back! But did you *ever* see such a size?'

'It's terrific, Theodosia,' I said. 'I was over nine feet when I returned. But he's twice that height.'

'But where are we going to put him?' she asked. 'None of these bedrooms is big enough – even if 'e could get through the door.'

'Well,' I said, 'we'll think up some way to manage. Let's get him comfortable where he is for the present.'

'Don't you think you ought to 'ave a doctor look at 'im, Master Tommy? I 'ad a sister once who came down with dropsy. Like an elephant she swelled up. But a doctor gave 'er some pills and she got all right.'

'Yes, Theodosia,' I said. 'I *would* feel happier if I had a doctor to keep an eye on him. And if I have to, I will. But so long as John Dolittle is conscious I know he would rather I didn't.'

'Doctor Pinchbeck, over to Oxenthorpe, is very good, they tell me,' said she. 'Now where are them blankets, Master Tommy?'

'In these cupboards here,' I said. 'Look, I'll load you up and then you send Matthew back to help me get these mattresses out. We're going to need three at least – maybe four.'

'All right,' she called, running down the stairs under a pile of bedclothes.

'And listen, Mrs Mugg,' I called after her.

'Don't let those animals fuss the Doctor with questions. Let him rest.'

Well, we got the poor man comfortably settled after a while. By placing four double-bed mattresses end to end we made a bed big enough for him, on the lawn beneath the elms. Then we got all the bolsters in the house, made them into a pile at one end, and covered them with a sheet. That was his pillow. I got him to roll over a couple of turns from where he sat; and there he was, safe in bed.

'It's pretty cool out here, Doctor,' I said. 'How many bedclothes do you think you'll need?'

He said he thought two thicknesses would be enough. So Theodosia got some carpet thread and by stitching four blankets into one piece, twice, she had two blankets big enough to spread over him.

'But listen, Tommy,' said Dab-Dab, 'what if it should rain? There are clouds over there to the south-west.'

'You're right,' I said. 'So there are. Let me see, I wonder what—'

'How about the circus tent?' said Gub-Gub. 'That's big enough to keep the rain off him.'

'Splendid!' I cried. 'Let's go and get it.' And off we all went towards the stable.

The big tent, a perfectly tremendous affair, was all that the Doctor had kept from his circus days. He had thought it might come in handy some time for housing larger animals in the zoo. It was stored in the hay-loft over the stable. It weighed I don't know how much. But I do know that it took all of our strength to drag it down out of the loft. But once we got it down, the old horse told us to hitch him on to one end of it with a rope and collar. Then he trailed it across the grass to where the Doctor lay.

We found that some of the poles were missing. But after we had sent Chee-Chee aloft in the trees to tie the ridge-ends to branches, we finally managed to get it strung up and pegged down somehow so that it would serve as a shelter over the bed.

'This is splendid, Tommy,' said Dab-Dab when we had finished. 'Because, you see, the tent is hidden here from the road by the house and trees. No one will suspect anything.'

'Yes,' I said, 'the Doctor can make this his bedroom till he has grown small again – the same as I did – and can live in the house. We'll have to get some furniture out for him later. But he won't need it yet. Now comes the question of food, Dab-Dab. Have we plenty of milk?'

'About three quarts,' said the housekeeper.

I asked Matthew to get me some oil-lamps. And after we had them lighted we went inside the tent.

For the present the Doctor seemed very comfortable. His breathing sounded a little better already. He drank up the three quarts of milk as if it had been no more than a glassful. I guessed that, as usual, he had been too busy getting ready to travel to bother about eating and had probably gone without food for many hours. I rigged up a place for myself to sleep beside him and told the others they could go to bed.

Presently he began to doze off again. But just before he fell asleep he murmured, 'Stubbins, see that the locust has a good feed of lettuce. He will be leaving again before daylight.'

'All right, Doctor,' I said. 'I'll attend to it.'

'And don't forget to unload all the baggage off him – some very important specimens, Stubbins, and a lot of notes – very important.'

'Yes,' I said, 'I'll get them unloaded and stored away safe.'

I took his pulse again, and while I was doing it he dropped off into a peaceful sleep.

# Chapter Nine
## THE MOON CAT

SEVERAL times during what was left of that night I heard John Dolittle stir. By the light of the turned-down lamp I went and looked at him quietly. It was when the first grey of dawn was showing through the canvas of the tent that he called to me. And as I bent over him I heard the great locust outside whirr up off the lawn and start its return journey to the Moon.

'Listen, Stubbins,' he said weakly. 'In the baggage you'll find a package done up in large orange-coloured leaves.'

'Yes, Doctor,' I said. 'I saw it. I have it stored safely away with the other things.'

He beckoned me to come nearer. Then he whispered in my ear, 'There's a cat inside it.'

I tried not to show my surprise. But I must say it was a shock. The Dolittle household had kept almost every kind of animal on Earth in its time, but never a cat. The Doctor always feared that it wouldn't get on happily with the birds and the others. But I only answered, 'Yes, Doctor.'

'I had to bring it, Stubbins,' he went on, 'simply had to. I found it on the far side of the Moon, in

the twilight zone. There was a whole colony of
them there. They were the one kind of animal
that refused to join in the Council's work for
balancing life and stamping out the everlasting
warfare of one species against another. You know
they're very independent, cats. Consequently
they had had to live by themselves. But when I
visited them they did not seem very happy just
the same.'

'But how did cats come to be on the Moon in the
first place?' I asked.

'Oh, I imagine there must have been a pair of
cats on that piece of the Earth which shot away
into the sky and became the Moon, thousands of
years ago. The same thing that happened to the
Moon Man himself. I made a lot of other discoveries, too, in the animal kingdom up there
after you left. I'll tell you all about them when I'm
feeling stronger.'

I was simply aching to ask him a thousand questions concerning these discoveries. But for his
sake I held my patience.

'All right, Doctor,' I said; 'there's no hurry.'

'No, but listen,' he said, dropping his voice to a
whisper again. 'Keep it quiet – about the cat.
Don't say anything to our own animals for the
present. It would just upset them. I'll speak to
them myself later on. She's a nice cat – quite a
character. You know most people think cats are
just stay-at-homes. They are not. They're very
adventurous. This one astonished me. Said that
Otho Bludge, the only man up there, didn't
understand cats. And she wanted to travel – to
see the world – the Earth down here where her

ancestors came from. Could she come with me? Well, what was I to do? She promised she would kill no birds, eat no mice and live on nothing but milk – if I'd only take her. You see, Stubbins, I just had to bring her. Polynesia made an awful row, but there was nothing else for it.'

'Very good, Doctor,' I said. 'I'll see she is fed regularly.'

But while I said the words I foresaw a revolution in the Dolittle household ahead of us.

'Now run and get breakfast,' said the Doctor. 'Look, it's daylight outside.'

Weary from the effort of talking, he sank back upon the pillow. It made me terribly unhappy to see him lying there so weak and weary. I had never known John Dolittle to have a single day's sickness in his life. He had always been so up-and-doing, cheerful, strong and active.

'Tell me,' I said, 'don't you think it would be a good idea if I got a doctor in to see you?'

'Oh, no, Stubbins,' he smiled. 'I'll be all right. You just keep note of my pulse. We don't want any medical men coming here. It might bring those newspaper fellows around.'

'Can I get you anything to eat?' I asked.

'Bring me a half-dozen eggs beaten up – with a little pepper and salt. But there's no hurry. Get your own breakfast first, Stubbins. I'll have another little sleep now. And don't forget the cat, will you?'

'No, Doctor,' I said, 'I won't forget.'

'By the way,' he added as I pulled aside the tent-flap to leave, 'you will find her difficult to talk to. Took me quite a while to get on to the language. Quite different from anything we've tried so far

in animal languages. A curious tongue – very
subtle, precise and exact. Sounds as though
whoever invented it was more anxious to keep
things to himself than to hand them over to
others. Not chatty at all. There's no word for
*gossip* in it. Not much use for people who want to
be chummy. Good language for lawyers though.'

When I got indoors I found every one sitting
down to a good breakfast which Dab-Dab and
Theodosia had prepared. I was glad to be able to
tell them that the Doctor could breathe and speak
better this morning, but that he still seemed very
weak and easily tired.

'The first thing,' I said, 'is to make him really
strong and well. After that we'll have to get his
weight and size down to what it was. But that
must be done gradually, without letting him lose
strength. I'll get him to lay out a diet for himself
– then we'll know just what things to give him
and what not to give him.'

'Then you ain't goin' to get another doctor to see
'im, Master Tommy?' asked Theodosia.

'No,' I said, 'not for the present anyhow.'

'What would he want with a doctor?' Gub-Gub
asked, raising his eyebrows. 'John Dolittle knows
all there is to be known, himself, about doctoring,
doesn't he?'

'Well,' I explained, 'you see, when doctors get ill
they sometimes have to get other doctors to doctor
them.'

'Humph!' grunted Gub-Gub. 'How extraordinary! Seems a dreadful waste of money.'

'Now,' I said, 'the main thing for the present –
you must forgive me if I repeat it – is that all of

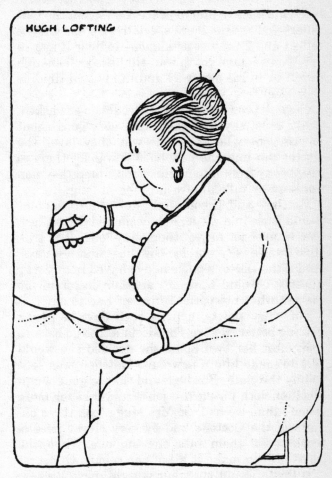

HUGH LOFTING

'Mrs Mugg took three suits and made them into one'

you, you, Gub-Gub, Jip, Whitey, Too-Too, everybody, must leave him in peace. Don't visit the tent
unless you're sent there specially. He has a lot to
tell us and I am just as anxious to hear it as you
are. But we have got to wait till he is well enough
to tell us in his own way and in his own time. Is
that clear?'

They all promised that they would do as I asked.
And I must say that they were very good about
it. Any one who knew the way they loved the
Doctor can imagine how hard it was for them to
keep away from him at this time, when they had
not seen or talked with him for so long.

Matthew and Theodosia I allowed into the tent
– and, once in a while, Polynesia and Chee-Chee.
But I never let any of them stay long. It is true
that I was a very worried boy those first few days.
And if the Doctor's pulse had behaved in any way
queerly I would have got another doctor in, no
matter what my patient himself had to say.

But, very slowly, a little each day, he began
getting better. Before Theodosia left to go back to
look after her own home she decided she would
like to make him a new suit. Matthew was sent
to buy the cloth. But he found that to get enough
woollen cloth for such a job would cost far more
money than we had. So Mrs Mugg took three old
suits of the Doctor's and by very clever needle-
work made them into one big one. Then she
re-dyed it to make it all of one colour. Of course
the Doctor could not wear it right away because
he was not yet well enough to move about. But he
was very glad to have it against the day when he
could get up.

# Chapter Ten
## THE DOLITTLE HOUSEHOLD REVOLUTION

I FOUND that the Doctor had given me a hard job when he told me not to let the other animals know about the cat. That same night I sneaked off quietly by myself and opened up the crate to feed her. I suppose I had expected to find an ordinary cat. But there was nothing ordinary about her. She had a long, thin, snaky sort of body and long thin legs – something like the Indian cheetah. And she was the wildest creature I had ever seen.

Most likely she had thought it was the Doctor coming to see her when I started to undo the wrapping on her cage. But when she saw a strange human looking in at her she bounded away from me and cowered, snarling, in a corner. I saw it was no use trying to coax her in that state of fear. I would have to let her get used to me gradually. So I put the bowl of milk down inside and closed up her crate. Soon I heard her lapping up the food hungrily and I tiptoed quietly away.

I thought it best to consult with Polynesia. I took her aside where we could talk without being heard.

'Listen, Polynesia,' I said, 'you know about this cat?'

She jumped as though I had stuck a pin in her.

'Young man,' she said severely, 'if you wish to remain a friend of mine don't ever speak of that animal by the usual word. Those *creatures* – well, just call it *It*!'

'Very well, Polynesia,' I said, 'we'll call her It – no, let's call her Itty, shall we?'

'Itty?' muttered the parrot with a frown. 'Itty? Kitty? *Pity* would be better. Oh, well, have it your own way.'

And from that time on the cat was called Itty.

'You see, Polynesia,' I said, 'this cat–'

'Don't use that word!' she screamed. 'It gets me all fluffed up.'

'Excuse me,' I went on. 'But Itty has to be fed on the quiet for the present. The Doctor doesn't want the other animals to know about her until he can tell them himself. But you can understand it isn't going to be easy for me to get meals to her. Now what I was going to ask you to do is this: when I want to go and give – er – Itty food, I'll make a sign to you. Then you lead the other animals off somewhere or keep them busy till I get back, see?'

The parrot agreed she would do this. And for a while the plan worked all right. Every day when I wanted to take milk to the cat, Polynesia would suggest to the animals that they should all go with her to see how the lettuce was coming up in the kitchen garden, or something like that. And the coast would be left clear for me to attend to Itty.

The cat began gradually to get used to my visits, and when she saw that I meant to do her no more harm than to bring her milk she actually became friendly in a strange awkward way.

However, the household finally got suspicious. Maybe Polynesia's excuses for getting them out of the way began to grow stale. Anyway, Gub-Gub asked me one evening what was the reason for my disappearing so mysteriously at the same hour every day. Then Too-Too, that bird with the keenest ears in the world, remarked that she had heard strange unearthly noises in the attic. (The attic was where I had stored the Doctor's moon baggage.) And finally Jip – who had been decorated with a golden dog collar for his cleverness in smelling – said he had sniffed a new queer scent on the upper stairs.

I began to get uncomfortable. I glanced across at Polynesia to see if I would get any help from her. But the old rascal was gazing up at the ceiling, humming a Danish sea song to herself, pretending not to hear a word of the conversation. Chee-Chee, the only other one in the secret, was frightfully busy clearing up the hearth, in hopes, no doubt, that he wouldn't be asked any questions. The white mouse was watching, silent, from the mantelpiece, his big pink eyes wide open with curiosity. I heard Dab-Dab through the open door to the pantry, drying dishes at the sink. I got more uncomfortable still.

'Tell me, Tommy,' said Jip, 'what's in all that baggage the Doctor brought down from the Moon?'

'Oh – er – plants,' I said, 'moon plants, and

seeds – no end of seeds, Jip; things the Doctor wants to try out down here on the Earth to see how they'll do.'

'But this wasn't any plant smell which I caught,' said Jip. 'It was something quite different.'

'What was it like?' asked Too-Too.

'Seemed like an animal,' said the dog.

'What kind of an animal?' asked the white mouse.

'I couldn't quite make out,' said Jip. 'It was very queer. It set the hair on my back all tingling. And I couldn't understand why. Is there nothing else but plants in that baggage, Tommy?'

For a long time I remained silent while all the animals watched me, waiting for an answer. At last Polynesia said, 'Oh, you might as well tell them, Tommy. They're bound to know sooner or later.'

'Very well, then,' I said. 'The Doctor had asked me not to say anything for the present. But I see it can't be helped. There's a cat in the baggage.'

Polynesia squawked at the hated word. Jip jumped as though he'd been shot. Too-Too let out a long low whistle. Dab-Dab in the pantry dropped a plate on the floor where it broke with a loud crash – the first time she had ever done such a thing in her life. Gub-Gub grunted with disgust. As for the white mouse, he uttered one piercing squeal and fainted dead away on the mantelpiece. I jumped up and dashed a teaspoonful of water in his face. He came to immediately.

'Gracious!' he gasped. 'Such a shock!'

'What,' I asked, 'the water?'

'No,' said he, 'the cat. Oh, how could he? How *could* the Doctor have done it?'

'The place will never be the same again,' groaned Too-Too.

'Oh, me, oh, my!' wailed Gub-Gub, shaking his head sadly. 'How awful!'

Dab-Dab stood in the pantry doorway, shaking with sobs. 'It can't be true,' she kept saying, 'it just can't be true.'

'A cat!' muttered Jip. 'I should have known! Nothing else could have made my spine tingle like that but the smell of a cat. Gosh! I'll chase her off the place.'

Then they all broke out together in a general uproar. Some were for going away at once, leaving the beloved home they had enjoyed so long. Some begged to be allowed to see the Doctor and ask him to send the animal away. Others, like Jip, swore they would drive her out. Panic, pandemonium and bedlam broke loose in the kitchen.

'Stop it!' I cried at last. 'Stop it! Now listen to me, all of you. You're just making a lot of fuss without knowing what you're talking about. You ought to know the Doctor well enough by now to be sure he would not bring anything here which will make any of you unhappy. I admit I'm not fond of cats in a general way myself – neither is Polynesia. But this cat is different. It's a moon cat. It may have all sorts of new ideas on cat behaviour. It may have messages for us. The Doctor is fond of it. He wants to study it.'

'But, Tommy,' squeaked the white mouse, 'our lives won't be safe for a moment.'

'Please be quiet, Whitey,' I said sharply. 'How many times have you heard John Dolittle say, "People as a race are the most selfish of all creatures"?'

'There's nothing as selfish as a cat,' put in Jip with a growl.

'How often,' I went on, 'have you heard him railing against people who are for ever spouting about glorious freedom while they deny it to animals? Are you going to be like that? You haven't met *this* cat. You know nothing about her. And yet you all start squawking like a lot of day-old chicks as soon as I mention her.'

'She'll have to wear a bell — she'll *have* to!' cried Dab-Dab. 'Cats when they come sneaking up in the dark just give me the heebee-jeebees. I couldn't stand it. I'd have to leave home — after all these years!'

She began to weep again.

'Calm yourself, Dab-Dab,' I said, '*please*! At least I expected some sense from you.' I turned to the others. 'This cat is a sport, every one must give her that credit. She trusted the Doctor enough to ask to be brought down to the Earth. Which of you would have the courage, if a stranger came down from the Moon, to ask to be taken away from this world and planted on another you had never seen? Answer me that.'

Rather to my surprise, my long high-sounding speech seemed to have quite an effect on them. When I ended there was a thoughtful silence. Presently Jip said quietly, 'Humph! You're right, Tommy. That certainly was plucky. She took a big gamble.'

'Now I'm going to ask you all,' I said, 'for the Doctor's sake, to treat this cat with kindness and consideration. You haven't got to like her if you can't. But at least let us be polite and fair to her.'

'Well,' said Dab-Dab with a sigh, 'I hope it will work out all right. But if she goes and has kittens in my linen cupboard I'll fly south with the first flock of wild ducks that passes over the garden, as sure as shooting!'

'Don't worry,' I said. 'Leave her to the Doctor. He'll know how to manage her. I can't even talk her language yet. She is still very shy and wild. But she'll fit in all right, once she gets used to us all.'

Little Chee-Chee the monkey, squatting by the hearth, spoke up for the first time. 'She's smart,' he said, 'a bit mysterious and queer – and independent as the dickens too – but mighty clever. Polynesia wouldn't bother to learn her funny language. But I picked up a few words of it.'

'And another thing,' I said, 'you need have no fears about her slaughtering other creatures. She has promised the Doctor not to kill birds and' – I glanced up at Whitey on the mantelpiece – '*not* to eat mice.'

'What's her name?' asked Gub-Gub.

'Her name is Itty,' I said.

'Humph!' murmured the white mouse thoughtfully. 'Itty, eh? Itty – pretty!'

'Are you trying to make up poetry, Whitey?' asked Gub-Gub.

'Oh, no,' said the white mouse, airily twirling his whiskers. 'That's just called doggerel.'

'*Whatterel?*' barked Jip in disgust.

'Doggerel,' said the white mouse.

'Cat-and-doggerel, I'd call it,' grunted Gub-Gub.

And they all giggled and went off to bed in a much better mood than I had hoped for.

# Chapter Eleven
## THE DOCTOR'S ACCIDENT

**B**Y the end of the week the Doctor was showing a great improvement in health. So far he had lived almost entirely on milk, eggs, and lettuce. These three foods seemed to strengthen him better than anything else. And it was a good thing that they did. Because we could not have afforded a more expensive diet. The lettuce, of course, cost practically nothing while we could grow it in the garden. (Gub-Gub and I planted several new beds if it.) Just the same, I was gladder than ever that I had my book-keeping job. I saved every penny I could out of the three shillings and sixpence a week, in case anything unexpected should turn up which might require a special lot of money.

I still slept in the Doctor's tent in case he should need anything during the night. One morning early he called me to him and said, 'Stubbins, I'm feeling pretty well. I think I'll try to get up today.'

'But, Doctor,' I said, 'are you sure you'll be strong enough?'

'No, I'm not sure,' he said. 'But the only way to

find out is to try. Help me into that suit which Theodosia made for me, will you?'

I was very anxious. At the same time I was very glad. I helped him on with his clothes, but when it came to helping him stand up and walk, I found I wasn't much use. Though I measured then something over five feet and a quarter, he had to bend down to reach my shoulder. And he was terribly afraid he might fall on me.

However, after I had cut a long walking-stick for him out of the forest, he managed to hobble around the tent pretty well. Then he got more adventurous still and wanted to go out into the garden. I did my best to persuade him not to but he tried it anyway. He actually got half-way across the lawn before he sank down from weariness.

The next day he did better still. It was strange to see his towering form walking about the turf, his head occasionally disappearing among the leaves of the high elm trees. This time after a few rests he said he would like to go as far as the zoo enclosure. And when he got to it he actually stepped over the ten-foot wall instead of bothering with the door.

After that he was impatient to get into the house. There was one door to the old building which was never used by us. Closed up for years now, its faded green paint and tarnished brass knocker faced towards the Long Lawn, the same as did the back door. But it was always known for some reason or other as the side door. The Doctor was sitting against one of the elms, staring at it while taking a rest.

'You know, Stubbins,' said he, 'I believe I could get through that door.'

'Oh, Doctor,' I said, 'why, it isn't half your height!'

'I didn't mean to try it standing up,' he said. 'But by lying down and sort of worming my way in I think I might manage it. You see, it's a double door. A very long time ago, before the days of my great-grandfather, they used to use that door for garden parties – in fact it was the main door. There was a drive running up to it too, close to the house, where the paeony beds are now. Just open it and take a few measurements for me, will you? It is my hips that will be the difficulty. If they'll go through the rest of me will.'

So I got the long garden tape and measured the width of the Doctor's hips. Then after hunting with Dab-Dab through all the drawers in the house I found the key to the side door. Its hinges creaked with age and rust as we swung both halves of it open.

I went back to the Doctor.

'It looks to me as if it should be all right,' I said, 'that is, as far as the width of the door-frame is concerned. But what are you going to do when you get inside?'

'Oh, the headroom of the hall there is extra high,' he said. 'Let's try it, Stubbins.'

Well, that was when we had our accident. By wriggling and squirming the Doctor got in – half-way. There he stuck. Dab-Dab was in a terrible state of mind. I pushed him to see if I could get him all the way in. Then I pulled at him to see if I could get him out. But I couldn't budge him either way. I had made a mistake of six inches in my measurements.

'We had better get some carpenters and workmen in, Tommy,' said Dab-Dab. 'We certainly can't leave him like this.'

'No, don't do that,' said the Doctor. 'You'll have the whole town here gaping at me. Get Matthew to come.'

So I sent off Too-Too to bring the cats'-meat-man to the rescue.

Matthew scratched his head when he saw the Doctor's legs sticking out into the garden and the other half of him inside the house.

'Well, now, wait a minute, Tommy,' said he. 'Yer see that fan-light window over the door? If you give me a saw and a ladder I can maybe cut away the 'ead of the door-frame.'

'But won't the bricks come tumbling down, then?' I asked.

'No, I don't think so,' said Matthew. 'The frame of the window-arch will 'old the wall up. Give me a saw. D'yer mind if I stand on top of you, Doctor?'

'Not a bit,' said John Dolittle. 'Only get me either in or out. Don't leave me as I am.'

I got a saw and Matthew – who was a very handy man with tools – climbed up on top of the Doctor and sawed away the door-head. This gave us, after we had got the glass out of the window, another foot and a half clearance. The Doctor squirmed and wriggled some more.

'Ah!' he said presently. 'I think I can manage now. But I'll have to go in, not out.'

We next drove a stake into the ground to give him something to push against with his feet. The rest of the animals stood around while, with much grunting and puffing, he finally forced the whole of his big body into the hall. He lay down with a sigh.

'Splendid,' he said, 'splendid!'

'But you can't sit up where you are, Doctor, can you?' I asked.

'Half a mo', Doctor,' said Matthew. 'Wait till I cut a 'ole in the ceilin'. We can put the boards back afterwards so no one would know the difference. Wait while I run upstairs. I'll 'ave you comfortable.'

The cats'-meat-man ran round by the kitchen stairs and soon we heard him sawing away at the floor above. Bits of plaster began falling on the Doctor but Chee-Chee and the white mouse cleared them off him as fast as they fell.

Before long a hole appeared in the hall ceiling big enough even for the Doctor's head to go through.

'Thank you, Matthew,' said John Dolittle. 'What would I do without you?'

He hoisted himself into a sitting position, and his head disappeared from my sight into the opening.

'Ah!' I heard him say with a sigh. 'Here I am, home at last! Upstairs and downstairs at the same time. Splendid!'

After he had taken a rest he managed to turn himself right around inside the hall. Then, facing the door once more, he tried to get *out* into the garden. It was a hard job. He got stuck again halfway.

'Listen, Doctor,' said the white mouse, 'and I'll

tell you what we mice do when we want to get through a specially small hole.'

'I wish you would!' said the Doctor, puffing.

'First you breathe in, deep,' said Whitey. 'Then you breathe out, long. Then you hold your breath. Then you shut your eyes and think that the hole is only half as big as it is. Of course if you're a mouse you think that a cat is coming after you as well. But you needn't bother about that. Try it. You'll see. You'll slide through like silk. Now, a deep breath – in, out – and don't forget to shut your eyes. Do it by feeling. Just imagine you're a mouse.'

'All right,' said the Doctor. 'I'll try. It's hard on the imagination, but it should be awfully good for my figure.'

Whether there was anything in Whitey's advice or not, I don't know. But, anyway, at the second attempt the Doctor got through all right and scrambled out on the lawn laughing like a schoolboy.

We were all very happy now that he could get both in and out of the house. Right away we brought in the mattresses from the tent under the trees and turned the big hall into a bedroom for him. He said he found it very comfortable, even if he did have to pull his knees up a bit when he wanted to sleep.

Before long, finding himself so much better, John Dolittle gave all his attention to bringing his size down to a natural one. First he tried exercise. We rigged up a heavy sweater for him made out of a couple of eiderdown quilts. And in this he ran up and down the Long Lawn before breakfast.

'He ran up and down the Long Lawn before breakfast'

His thundering tread shook the whole garden till the dishes rattled on the pantry shelves and the pictures began falling from the walls in the parlour.

But this did not thin him down fast enough to satisfy him. Someone suggested massage. So we laid him out on the lawn and Matthew, Chee-Chee and I pummelled and pounded him for hours. He said it reminded him of the time when the elephant fell sick in the circus and he and all the crew had climbed aboard the animal with ladders to rub the pains out of it, till everybody had to stop with stiff muscles.

Gub-Gub asked why we didn't use the lawn-roller on him. But we decided this would be a little too drastic.

'Why don't you try it on yourself, Gubby?' Jip said. 'Your figure could do with a little taking down, too.'

'What's the matter with my figure?' said Gub-Gub, gazing down at his ample curves. 'Why, I wouldn't change it for anything!'

It proved to be a slow business for the poor Doctor, this getting back to ordinary size. But he certainly kept at it with a will. And soon with the diet, the exercise and the massage (besides, of course, the change of climate and gravity) he began to look more like himself.

# Chapter Twelve
## THE MOON MUSEUM

**B**UT all of us, including John Dolittle, saw that it was still probably a matter of some weeks before he would be able to carry on a usual life the same as other people. He could not yet pass through an ordinary door without going down on all fours; he could not sit in the biggest armchair without the arms breaking off; he could not grasp a common pencil or pen in his huge fingers and make it write properly.

This annoyed him greatly. He was so eager to get at his notes. He planned to write a new book, a book about the Moon.

'It will be the greatest thing I have ever done, Stubbins,' he said, 'that is, of course, if I make a good job of it. And even if I don't, it will at least contain information of great value for future writers on natural history.'

I, too, of course was very keen for him to get at those notes. Being his secretary I should have to help him and so would get a glimpse of what studies and experiments he had made. But Dab-Dab was of quite another mind about it.

'Tommy,' she said, 'there's no hurry about that

book he wants to write. I don't mean to say it isn't
important – though, for my part, I can't see much
sense in mixing up the Moon and the Earth, as
though life weren't mixed up enough as it is for
simple country folk. But the main thing is this:
you know how he is – once he gets started on a
new line of work he goes at it like a crazy man,
night and day; doesn't stop for meals; doesn't stop
for sleep; nothing but work. He isn't strong
enough yet for that sort of thing. For pity's sake
keep him away from those notes – at least till he
is perfectly well.'

As a matter of fact, there was no urgent need
at present for the housekeeper's fears. The Doctor
himself saw that there was not much sense in his
attempting to write a long book until he could
move round his study without upsetting things,
or smashing delicate laboratory apparatus with
clumsy experiments.

By daytime he contented himself with exercis-
ing and with some gardening. He had brought
many different sorts of seeds with him from the
Moon, also roots of plants. He wanted to see if
these could be grown in our world, and what differences they would show in new climate and conditions. Some were vegetables and fruits, good to
eat. In these, of course, Gub-Gub was especially
interested; and he immediately started to keep
notes on his own account, planning to make a new
volume for his famous Encyclopedia of Food. This
volume was to be called *Moon Meals*.

With the pig's assistance the Doctor and I
planted rows and rows of new and strange-shaped
seeds.

In that great bulk of baggage which he had brought down with him were also the eggs and grubs of insects: ants, bees, water-flies, moths and what-not. These had to have special hatching-boxes made for them, so they could be kept warm during cool nights; while others had to be planted in proper places in the garden, among grasses or trees, where they would be likely to find food and conditions to their liking.

Then again, he had brought sacks full of geological specimens; that is, rocks, pieces of marble, something that looked like coal and all manner of samples out of the hand-made mines he had dug in the mountains of the moon. Among them were pieces that had precious stones in them – or what looked like precious stones – pebbles and crystals that could have been opals, sapphires, amethysts and rubies. And fossils he had too – shells of curious snails, fishes, lizards and strange frogs that no longer lived either on Earth or Moon – all turned now to stone as hard as flint.

To take care of these we added another department to the Doctor's many-sided establishment. We called it the Moon Museum. In a disused harness-room of the big stable I set up shelves round the walls and even showcases with glass tops. And here were placed all the fossils and geological specimens along with some very beautiful pressed flowers and leaves which had also come down in the baggage.

Jip suggested that I should put the cat there, in a glass case too – so that she wouldn't get hurt.

I was very proud of my job when it was done.

I must say it did look like a regular museum; and the Doctor was no end pleased with its workmanlike, scientific appearance.

'You have a real gift for order and neatness in these things, Stubbins,' he said. 'That's the trouble with me – never could be orderly or neat. My sister Sarah – she used to be housekeeper for me, you know – she was always at me about my untidiness. In fact that's why she left me to go and get married. Poor dear Sarah, I wonder how she's getting on. An excellent woman – in many ways. But this, Stubbins, this is splendid! And you've done it all yourself. What would I do without you?'

As I have said, I had been careful not to ask him questions about the Moon until he wished to speak of it himself. I am proud of my own patience in this, for any one can imagine how keen I was to learn how he had at last got away from the Moon Man – and a thousand other things besides.

So far he had said little or nothing of his last months in that other world. But it was natural that in our talks after supper he would sooner or later get started. And at last one evening he did.

'By the way, Stubbins,' said he, 'what became of Bumpo? He was here with you when I left. Where is he now?'

'He was gone before I got down from the Moon, Doctor,' I said. 'He left messages for us with Matthew. It seems he wanted to go back to Oxford to visit some of his old friends and perhaps to take up some new studies there too. He couldn't tell just how long he would be gone. But he said he

would certainly come and visit you again before
he went back to Africa.'

'Well, I'm glad of that,' said the Doctor. 'Fine
fellow, Prince Bumpo, one of the best.... Yes, yes.
There have been many times when I don't know
what I would have done without him. But tell me,
Stubbins, do you remember how long it took the
Giant Moth to bring you down?'

'Not exactly, Doctor,' I answered. 'Passing
through the dead belt, I got awfully sick, dazed
and mixed up. And then my mind was so full of
worry about having left you up there alone, I
don't know that I should have remembered
anyway.'

'Humph!' said he thoughtfully. 'It's a pity you
can't remember. I wanted to make a little calcula-
tion between the speed of your moth and that of
my locust – that is for the downward journey. But
you have no cause to blame yourself for leaving
me. You never had a chance to do anything else.
You see, the Moon Man, Otho Bludge, wanted to
get rid of you: but he wanted to keep me. I had
quite a time with him when I wanted to get back
here. That is after–'

I interrupted him. I knew something interesting was coming – that at last he was going to
speak of how he got away. Many more ears
besides mine wanted to hear that story.

'Pardon me, Doctor,' I said. 'But would you mind
if I got the animals in, so they can listen? I know
they are all longing to hear what happened after
I left you.'

'Why, yes, certainly,' he said. 'Bring them in by
all means. As a matter of fact, I meant to have

told you all, before this, about my last days up there. But I have been talking those moon languages for such a long time, I found I had grown sort of rusty and hesitating in speaking the languages of my own world. But they are coming back to me now and I think I can manage all right — that is, if you don't mind my speaking slowly.'

'Of course, Doctor,' I said as I got up, 'we understand that. But you will promise not to overtire yourself, won't you? Send us all away the first minute you feel weary.'

He said he would. And I ran out into the garden to go round to the kitchen. In the dusk on the lawn I bumped into Matthew Mugg, who had just arrived to pay John Dolittle a visit.

'The Doctor's going to tell us how he got off the Moon, Matthew,' I said. 'Would you like to come and listen?'

'You bet I would, Tommy,' said he. 'But of course if he talks in them animal lingos I won't understand the same as what you will. Never mind, you can explain to me afterwards. But I wouldn't miss it for anything. No, you bet I'll come!'

Then I ran on and found the animals gathered round the big fireplace in the kitchen. Here I spied another visitor, Cheapside. The sparrow had 'popped over' from London to hear the latest news of his old friend. They all let out a whoop of joy when I told them that at last they were going to hear the tale they had waited for so long.

And so, with two guests added to our own company, it was quite a circle that gathered round the Doctor that night. I had brought pencil and notebooks with me. For some months back I had been studying shorthand. And I was anxious to see if I could take down his words as fast as he spoke them.

'Ah!' whispered the white mouse, tittering with eager excitement as he settled down to listen, 'Tommy, this is like old times!'

# PART II

# Chapter One
## WHY JOHN DOLITTLE STAYED SO LONG ON THE MOON

'WELL,' the Doctor began, 'before you came in I was telling Stubbins here that I had quite a difficult time getting away from Otho Bludge, the Moon Man. But since you all want to listen to the story I had better begin at the beginning – that is, from where Stubbins was carried off by the moth and taken away. You know of course why that was. The Moon Man, who had bird spies in every corner of that world up there, heard that I was uneasy about Stubbins – or rather about his mother and father. The young rascal hadn't even told his parents he was going to the Moon – just stowed away aboard the moth without even my knowing it. Of course I feared his parents would be terribly worried, when he no longer came to visit them.

'These bird spies overheard us talking about this one night in our camp and they told Otho Bludge. Now I had been treating him for rheumatism, and he didn't want to lose me, it seemed. He thought if he got Stubbins back to the Earth I would no longer worry about him and

would be willing to stay. So he kidnapped the boy
and shipped him off before I had a chance to say
a word about it one way or the other.

'At first it was a great load off my mind. I knew
the trip could be made in safety – although, to be
sure, it was a hard and trying one. When the
moth got back and reported that he had landed
Stubbins on the Earth I was very happy. I admit
I was terribly sorry to lose him. And, no doubt, I
would have felt awfully lonely up there if I had
not been so busy.

'I have never known any one single year in my
whole life when so many interesting things for
study were presented to me at once. The days
never seemed long enough. There were great
portions of the Moon which Stubbins and I had
not yet even explored. I found new lakes with all
sorts of strange life in the waters. High in the
mountains, among the old craters of dead
volcanoes, I found fossil remains of different
animals which had thrived on the Moon long,
long ago and since died out – become extinct, as
we call it. Then there were the rocks at lower
levels. Comparing these with what I knew of our
own rocks down here, I was able to calculate the
exact age of the Moon – that is, I could tell within
a few thousand years, just when it was that the
great explosion occurred – the explosion which
shot the Moon off from the Earth and made it into
a separate little world, revolving around us in the
heavens.'

The Doctor paused a moment and turned to
Chee-Chee.

'By the way, Chee-Chee,' said he, 'now that

we're back, don't forget to remind me to alter that
chapter in my book on Monkey History.

'You mean the part about the story my grand-
mother told when I was little?' asked the monkey.

'Oh, I remember that,' cried the white mouse.
'It was called *The Days Before There Was a
Moon.*'

'That's right,' said the Doctor. 'The legend of
how a man, a prehistoric artist, was shot away
from the Earth the day before the Moon appeared
in the sky for the first time. I put it into my book,
even if it was only a story. But it now appears
that it was all practically true.

'If Otho Bludge had not been shot away by the
great explosion, life on the Moon today could
never have been what it is. It was he who saved
the animal world up there from dying out. He told
me it took him a long time to see what was going
to happen. Some of the larger creatures – great
prehistoric beasts that went off so suddenly with
him – some in egg-form like dinosaurs and such
– began eating up the plant life so fast that the
entire vegetable kingdom could hardly keep up
against the destruction. Of course all this, you
understand, took thousands and thousands of
years. But at last, when Otho had had enough
time to get himself used to his new surroundings,
he began to ponder over what should be done
about it. He had then grown immensely big. And
though he wasn't much good at arithmetic and
astronomy he saw the planets, the Sun and the
Earth revolving around him in the heavens and
he finally realized that he had already lived a
terribly long while.'

'About how long?' asked Gub-Gub.

'It's hard to say exactly,' said the Doctor. 'But certainly dozens of times longer than he knew people usually lived on the Earth. It must have been something in the vegetable diet, and of course the climate, lighter gravity and other things peculiar to that new world. It looked to him, he told me, as if life could go on up there pretty nearly for ever – *provided it was properly taken care of.*'

I whispered a word of explanation in Matthew's ear at this point. He nodded and winked back at me understandingly.

'And so,' the Doctor went on, 'Otho Bludge made up his mind that *he* would see to it that life *was* properly taken care of – life of both kinds, animal and plant. First he went round the whole of the Moon, exploring it many times, so that there was hardly a square yard of it that he hadn't examined. In a crude rough way he made a list of all the different forms of animals, insects, trees, shrubs and plants that he found. Knowing how long he had lived and how long he was likely still to live, he felt there was no need for hurry and he made a very complete job of it.'

'Humph! Must 'ave been quite a naturalist 'imself,' Cheapside put in.

'Yes, he most certainly was,' said the Doctor. 'A very great naturalist, rather the way that Long Arrow was, the man that we found in Spider-monkey Island. He didn't use science such as we use. But he gathered a tremendous lot of information and showed a remarkable common sense in what he did with it. Well, having listed all his

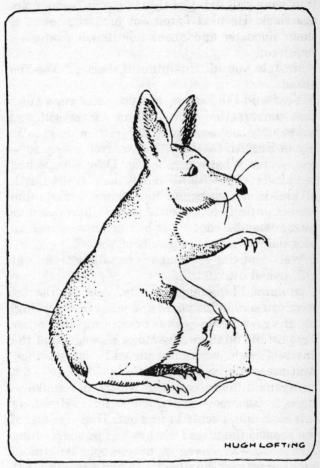

' "Oh, I remember that," cried the white mouse'

animals and plants – or, I should say, all that
they were still living at the time – he began upon
the work. He next found out just what each of
them lived on and about how much food each
required.'

'He told you all this himself, Doctor?' Too-Too
asked.

'Yes,' said the Doctor, 'but you must remember
that conversation between him and myself was
not exactly the same thing as Matthew and I talking in English together. No, no. Not nearly so –
er – exact. Whatever language Otho Bludge had
used in talking with his fellow men on the Earth
of prehistoric days, he had, when I met him,
almost entirely forgotten. After all, how could he
have remembered it – not having another human
to speak with for thousands of years?'

'Well, how did you manage to talk with him at
all?' asked Jip.

'In animal languages, mostly,' said the Doctor.
'For, you see, in his years and years of observing,
counting, watching and examining the other
forms of life up there, the Moon Man saw that the
animals could communicate with one another.
And presently be began, little by little, to catch
on to the different ways in which they spoke –
signs, noises, movements, and so forth. How long
this took him, I couldn't find out. That was one of
the great difficulties I always had in questioning
him – he was so vague, hazy, about lengths of
time, quantities, numbers – in fact anything that
had to do with figures. It was curious, because the
cleverness of the man was in all other matters
most astonishing.'

'Well, but, Doctor,' said Too-Too, 'wouldn't that be because he had lived so long?'

'Exactly,' said John Dolittle. 'He had lived many hundreds of our lifetimes. So, in some ways, his mind, his experience, was – well, he was like hundreds of men rolled into one, if you know what I mean. Then again, he had kept his attention on just a few subjects. Life in the Moon is a very simple matter – as it would be anywhere else where there were no human beings to make it complicated – er – you know, fussy, hard and mixed up.'

'Were the animals' languages on the Moon anything like the animal languages down here?' asked Gub-Gub.

'They were and they weren't,' said the Doctor. 'Of course they had all sprung from the languages of the Earth creatures. But after so long up there the birds and the rest of them spoke quite differently. Of course my own knowledge of animal languages helped me greatly in talking with them. But I found it dreadfully difficult at first. The words and phrases had nearly all changed. Only the manner, the way, of speaking remained.

'But this will show you how hard Otho Bludge himself must have worked: he discovered, without any education in natural history at all, the great part which the insects, like bees, play in the life of the plants. He knew all about it. I found that his knowledge of insect languages, even down to the water-beetles, was tremendous – far and away better than my own. And from that he went on to learn the languages of the vegetable world.'

'The language of vegetables!' cried Gub-Gub.

'Well,' said the Doctor, 'not exactly the languages of potatoes and carrots. We hadn't any up there. The expression "vegetable world" takes in anything that grows in the ground — trees, flowers, vines. Otho Bludge was the first naturalist to make any discoveries in this field of study. I had often wondered, years ago, if our plants down here had any way of talking to one another. I am still wondering.

'But up there, with a very much smaller animal kingdom, and entirely different conditions, certain kinds of trees and plants had worked out and developed languages of their own. You see, in this world, we are always mixing up breeds — crossing different sorts of dahlias to make new kinds, grafting fruit-trees, and even sticking rosebuds on to raspberry canes to make roses grow on a raspberry root. That's called a hybrid. How could we expect such a mixture to know what language to talk. Poor thing doesn't even know whether he's a raspberry or a rose!'

'Yes, most confusin', I should say,' Cheapside put in.

'But in the Moon,' said the Doctor, 'left to themselves for thousands of years, with no human hands to get them mixed up, the plants were much freer to work out things for themselves. Well, Otho Bludge thought out his plan and started off to try it. He did not want to interfere in the freedom of anything, but only to stop them all from interfering with the freedom of one another — to keep them from fighting and getting killed off. And that, when I got there, he

had very thoroughly succeeded in doing. It must
have been a terrifically hard thing – but then we
must remember that *he* was not interfered with
by any of his own kind either. I doubt very much
if it could ever have happened in our world. But,
remember again, his was a far smaller world –
easier to manage. At the beginning when he
explained his plan to the animals, the insects and
the plants, he found that not all of them were
pleased with the idea.'

'Why, did they go on fighting and eating one
another up?' asked Gub-Gub.

'Yes,' said the Doctor. 'But all parts of a world,
no matter what its size or kind, have to work
together. And those that would not help the
safety of others very soon found themselves in a
bad way – crowded out or starved out. Later
Bludge told them he wanted to form what he
called the Council. It was a parliament or con-
gress. Members of both the animal and the vegetable kingdoms came to it. They arranged everything that affected life on the Moon. Anybody
could get up and speak in this council or give
advice or make a complaint. Otho Bludge, the
Moon Man, was president. And after a while they
practically all saw that Bludge was right. It was
clear to them that he had brains, and they
accepted him as the leader, as the guide, in form-
ing a new and properly balanced world where
everything could live happily – more happily –
without fighting.'

# Chapter Two
## THE NATURALISTS' PARADISE

'AND so you see,' the Doctor went on, 'for quite a while after Stubbins left I was kept very busy learning more and more about this strange new state. It fascinated me. I had never seen anything like it before. I saw at once that while the Moon Man had done so much, there was a lot left for me to do too. I assure you I had no conceit about that. Beside this other human, as old and experienced as the Moon herself, I felt like a very humble little creature. But I had something of science which he had not; my mind was trained to make deductions, to reason – from my own experiences and those of others – as well as from history, human history, geological history, natural history.

'And besides wishing to help Otho Bludge – which I think I did do with scientific and medical advice – I began to wonder more and more how much of this new way of living could be brought about in my own home world, the Earth. I will speak of that again later. But the first thing I gave my attention to in this connection was the foods of the Moon.'

'Ah!' said Gub-Gub, sitting up.

'There were many members of the pumpkin family – melons, calabashes, squashes, luffas, marrows, cucumbers and what not. Most of them were good to eat. But any one who picked a ripe fruit had to keep one of its seeds after he had eaten it. That was a law made by the Council.

'Well, again by questioning Otho and, later, by talking with the moon creatures directly, I learned that certain members of the moon pumpkin family were terribly fattening. Not only just flesh-making, but they made your whole figure – bones and all – taller, wider and deeper. You became a giant if you didn't look out. It was quite clear that only a few living things on the Moon had stayed the same size as they are on the Earth. It was almost impossible to avoid growth to some extent up there. The poor Moon Man himself had become a giant, and he remained a giant. But he told me that at one time he was much bigger than he was when I met him. Some of the foods were much more fattening than others. Stubbins and I sprouted up like beanstalks the first few weeks we were there. Otho, however, was able to give me lists of certain foods which he had found the best for keeping your size down as much as possible.

'Next I turned my attention to the length of life on the Moon. This was most interesting, but often I was very puzzled when it came to getting any definite information about ages. From weeks and weeks of study I came to the conclusion that nearly all kinds of life as I saw them up there had stayed the same for many thousands of years.

Certain kinds, like the whispering vines and the singing trees, were much older than the rest.

'For quite a while after that I just had an awfully good time. I asked myself, 'Why bother about returning to the Earth? This is a naturalists' paradise. Adding your scientific knowledge to what Otho Bludge has done here will keep you busy all your days. And what better work could you be employed in? Keep the Moon Man in good health; cure his rheumatism for him whenever he falls ill; and just go on this way. Why worry? Maybe you, John Dolittle, will yourself live for ever – or anyhow as long as the Moon lives, which will probably be many thousands of years yet.' That's what I said to myself.

'But after a while I began to wonder – to wonder and wonder, about something. And about this something I started to take notes. By the way, Stubbins, on the note-taking I missed you badly. You had done it for me so long, you know. But Polynesia here was my salvation.'

'But how? She can't keep notes,' snorted Gub-Gub.

'No,' laughed the Doctor, 'but she has a memory that is often better than any notebook. It's almost like a letter-box you drop things into. You tell her to remember something when you're experimenting and she will always be able to fish it up out of her old head when you ask for it again later. I don't know what I would have done without her.'

Polynesia cocked one eye at the ceiling, twisted her head a couple of times and tried hard not to look pleased by the Doctor's flattery. Then she said, sighing, 'Ah, well, that's the difference between people and parrots. People when they get old say they can remember things in their childhood quite plainly – the things far off. But those that happened only yesterday, the things near to now, they can hardly remember at all. You talk about long life in the Moon, Doctor: what about me? I'm a hundred and eighty years old – and how much more, I'm not telling. How much longer I'll live, I don't know. Maybe I'm only a child yet myself, and that's why I'm as good as a notebook for remembering. Anyway, when I met King Charles hiding in the oak tree in England, he was trying to remember how many soldiers he had seen chasing him – awful scared he was, talking to himself, you know. And I – oh, well, it doesn't matter. I mustn't interrupt you, Doctor. Go on with the story.'

'The thing for which I now started to keep notes,' said the Doctor, 'was how much of this well-regulated, smoothly running world could be copied down here among us. The thought kept coming back to me, stronger and stronger each time. Always, even when I was an ordinary doctor and took care of people, natural history – animals, insects, plants, trees, fossils, rocks – had been my hobby. That hobby had become my life. And yet any one who studies natural history must come to fear sooner or later that all life faces a losing game down here with us.'

'Excuse me, Doctor,' said the white mouse, 'but I don't understand what you mean.'

'Life keeps on killing life,' said the Doctor. 'Don't you see? The fly is swallowed by the fish; the fish is eaten by the duck; the duck is devoured by the fox; the fox is slaughtered by the wolf. The wolf is shot by the human. And then humans – the only ones on top in our world – turn round and kill one another in war.'

There was a short silence. Dab-Dab had brought a pile of linen with her (the housekeeper always kept herself busy, even when listening to a story). She was turning over a stack of table napkins, looking for tears and holes.

'I told you that, Doctor,' she said quietly, 'long ago, when you wanted to start your Country House for House Flies.'

'Yes, yes,' said the Doctor, frowning thoughtfully. 'My idea with that was that if I gave the house flies a house for themselves – full of sugar, you know, and all that – maybe they would leave people's houses alone. It didn't work. They ate up all the sugar and came back to my house. But there you are, Whitey: that's what I mean. It's a losing game. Any naturalist who tries to save one kind of creature in our world finds out sooner or later that he is taking away the food from some other blessed creature – or making life impossible for himself. I had never had anything against the house flies, except that they would tickle the back of my neck when I was trying to write. And, as a medical man, I knew that they carry germs of disease. But they don't mean to. They're merely going about their own business like the rest of us.'

'They're a pest,' said Dab-Dab, laying aside a napkin that needed mending.

'Oh, quite, quite,' said the Doctor. 'But I'm sure they have some good in them somewhere – though I confess it's pretty hard to find. But you can all very well see, can't you, that when I found a world which was run along sensible lines, where no kind of life trod on the toes of any other kind of life, I began to wonder if something of those ideas could not be brought home and started here. That accounts for the note-taking, those bundles and bundles of palm-leaf paper which made up such a large part of my baggage, Stubbins. It is out of those notes that I will write my book.'

'There's plenty of time for that, Doctor,' sighed Dab-Dab. She spread out a woollen antimacassar eaten full of holes. 'Moths!' she hissed in disgust, and threw it aside.

# Chapter Three
## OTHO BLUDGE'S PRISONER

'NOW, all this time,' the Doctor, continued, 'the Moon Man was calling me in every so often to treat him for his rheumatism. I had fitted up a sort of makeshift laboratory for myself. Of course I had not many chemicals. All the medicines I had with me were what I had brought in the little black bag. But I had found a whole lot of useful drugs and things in the trees and rocks – such as quinine, zinc for making zinc ointment, and a whole lot more.

'Well, although my laboratory was a very rough and poor one, I was soon able to find out how to deal with his trouble. He was eating too much starch, for one thing. I changed his diet. I compounded some medicines for him. So long as he did what I told him, he got along very well. In fact, in the end I fancy I knew more about moon foods and what they did to the human body than he did.

'There was one special kind of melon he was very fond of. It was called goy-goy. This I had found was very bad for him. I had told him not to eat it. But, like a child – he was very childlike in many ways – he just wouldn't leave it alone. Finally I got quite severe with him. I ordered him not to touch it. He promised he wouldn't. But the next time he called me in about his rheumatism I saw, by the peelings that lay around him, that he had been eating goy-goy again.

'Well, this was when I was wondering if I could carry down to the Earth some of those sensible ideas about diet, long life and peaceful living which had panned out so well in the Moon. I saw no reason why they shouldn't work with us – partly, at all events. I was a little homesick too, I imagine. Anyway I was anxious to get down here and start experimenting with those ideas.

'So when, for the sixth or seventh time, Otho sent for me to attend to him – and again I found that he had been eating the forbidden goy-goy – I began to wonder if my staying on the Moon any longer would be of much use. I especially felt this way now, because I had nearly completed my observations of the Moon's seasons. The Moon, you see, revolves in a small circle round the Earth once a month; while the Earth, carrying the Moon with it, swings in a much bigger ring around the Sun, once a year. The Moon, hanging on to Earth, as it were, in this long journey would be bound to show effects and differences, not only with her own changing seasons, but with ours too. I particularly wanted to make some observations at the Earth's equinoxes – that is, in our spring and autumn. This of course meant staying up there a whole year. That year was now nearly over.

'Very well, then: this time Otho Bludge was a pretty sick Moon Man. And I realized that no matter how much medicine I gave him, sooner or later it would have no effect on him whatever — as long as he would go on eating goy-goy.

'So I got still more severe with him. I gave him a terrific lecturing. "I can do nothing with you," I said, "if you won't obey my orders. And anyway, very soon now I must go back to the Earth. I have promised my people that I will set off a smoke signal — the same as you did when you sent the moth for me — to let them know that I am coming. I shall expect you, when the time comes for me to leave, to help me in every way you can. After all, it was you who wanted me to come up to the Moon. And this, I feel, is the least you can do."

'He said nothing in answer. But I could see that he was not pleased with the idea at all. I left a small bottle of medicine with him and went away to go on with my studies and note-taking. Polynesia told me that the bird spies were watching me again — though I can't see why Otho Bludge bothered with that. There was no possible chance of my getting off the Moon unless I had his permission and his help. However, Polynesia — clever bird, I really don't know what I would have done without her — Polynesia started spying on the spies. And with her help I was kept just as well informed about Otho's doings as he was about what I was doing. However I was too busy with my observations on the moon seasons to bother about much else for the time being.

'At last the year was over and my notes were complete. I felt very glad. No one had ever seen the Moon's seasons, from the Moon, before. I had stacks and stacks of notes on temperatures, sunlight and earthlight with their effects on the animal and vegetable kingdoms, air pressures, rainfall and goodness knows how much more. I was packing up the last of these when word came to me that the Moon Man was not feeling so well and would I come to see him.

'This time I decided I would be more than severe. The moment had come for me to put my foot down. I gave him some medicine. And I stayed with him several nights until I had him in good health again. Then I said, "Listen, Otho Bludge, I want to go back to the Earth. I want to go now. I feel I have done all I can here. Will you please help me to set off the signal and return home?" Again he did not answer at once – he often thought a long while before he spoke. At last he said, "No, John Dolittle, I will not let you go. I need you here!"

'I was dumbfounded. The thought had never occurred to me that he would refuse my request – yet I don't know why it shouldn't have done. First I tried to argue with him. I explained how unfair this was. I reminded him again that it was he who had brought me up there – for his own purposes. This made no effect on him. Then I got angry. But it was no use. He was determined to keep me. I left him and went away very puzzled.

'Then for some weeks I wandered and wandered around the Moon, wondering what I should do. But the more I thought it over the more difficult the situation seemed. It looked now as though I was going to become a citizen of the Moon for good, whether I liked it or not. But with all the plans I had in mind I must confess I was very much annoyed.

'Then Polynesia one day had an idea. She said it was quite possible of course for Otho Bludge to keep me – as well as herself and Chee-Chee – prisoners on the Moon, but it was *not* possible for him to make me doctor him if I didn't want to. This sounded like good sense. And the next time the Moon Man sent word to me that he was suffering from rheumatism I refused to go to him.

'Again he sent me a message. He was very ill, he said. And again I sent back word that I would not come to help him until he was willing to help me. But it seemed he could be just as stubborn as I. No further message came to me.

'Then, I confess, I began to get worried. What if Otho Bludge should die? It was not that I was afraid that that would ruin my chances of getting away. I had done a lot for many of the birds and insects up there, curing them of different illnesses from which they suffered occasionally. And Polynesia said she was sure that they would do anything they could for me, even flying me back to the Earth, once the Moon Man was out of the way and they need no longer be afraid of disobeying his orders. But – well, once a doctor, always a doctor, I suppose. No physician, if he feels that his services may save someone's life – and there is no one else there – can stand aside and refuse to help.

'Maybe if the Moon Man had sent more messages I should have acted differently. But he didn't. That was the worst of it. Not another word came from him. We – Polynesia, Chee-Chee and I –

had moved our camp over to the far side of the Moon, the side you never see from the Earth: and I was trying to study the music of the singing trees. This had presented some problems in harmony which I was anxious to get to the bottom of.

'But suddenly the trees refused to sing any more. I could understand their language by then and I asked them why. They would tell me nothing. They remained silent. The same with the whispering vines. The birds, who did most of the spying for Otho, had disappeared. I tried talking with the insects – bees and the like; they wouldn't tell me anything either. I got more and more worried. It seemed as though the whole of the moon life was determined to be silent. It gave me a creepy sort of feeling. I began to wonder if they were all waiting for Otho Bludge to die – expecting it every minute.

'At last I couldn't bear it any more. I knew that if Otho – the man who had done something no human has ever done before – if Otho were to die I would never forgive myself. I was lying in bed, tossing and turning, trying to sleep. I jumped up. "Polynesia," I said, "I am going to him. I've got to!" She just swore in Swedish but did not try to stop me. I packed the black bag and left camp alone.

'I had a long way to go. I started off in darkness. But I knew that soon I would see the Earth rise and would have light from it to travel by. I never hurried so in all my life. How many hours the journey took me I don't know. My great fear was that I might be too late. When at last I began to get round on to the near side – the side of the

' "Polynesia," I said, "I am going to him. I've got to!" '

Moon you see from here — the going was easier
and I broke into a run. Soon I saw Otho's hut in
the distance. I call it a hut, but it was really a
very big house made of leaves. Gathered about it
there was a great crowd of birds, insects and some
animals, — all waiting in silence in the grey of the
earthlight. I pushed my way in. Otho Bludge was
lying on a bed with his eyes closed.'

# Chapter Four
## THE GENTLEMAN IN
## THE MOON

'I RUSHED to his bedside.

' "Otho, Otho!" I cried. He did not stir. He was unconscious. I felt his pulse. It was fast and jumpy. I got a thermometer out of the bag. His temperature was high – far too high. His rheumatism had run into complications – probably some form of rheumatic fever.

'I worked over him for hours. I knew if I did not bring the temperature down soon, this by itself would kill him. I got cold water and soaked big leaves in it. I plastered these all over his body and, by fanning him, I did manage to get the temperature lower by several degrees. I realized I had only got there just in time to save his life.

'It seems funny, when I look back on it now. There I was working like a slave to save the life of the man who meant to hold me a prisoner! Yet I did not think of it then. The only idea that filled my mind was that I, as a physician, must leave no stone unturned to keep him from dying.

'At last, after I had given him a heart stimulant with the hypodermic needle, he became conscious. Weakly he opened his eyes and looked at me. He said nothing. There came a curious, ashamed sort of expression into his face as he recognized who I was – that it was I who was working to save him. Presently he fell off into a peaceful sleep. I took his pulse again. While it was still fast, it was ever so much better and quite steady. I knew that the worst was over. I told one of the birds to call me as soon as he woke up. Then I curled up on the floor of his hut to get some sleep myself. As I dozed off I felt more at peace in my mind than I had done for many hours.

'I stayed with him I don't know how long – maybe four or five days. During all that time he never spoke. At the end, when I was about to leave him, he was quite well again, but still weak. I gave him the usual instructions as to what he should do. It was hardly necessary, for he had heard them many times before. I fastened up my medicine-bag and turned towards the open door of his hut.

'The Sun was shining on the beautiful moon-scape. You know how it looked, Stubbins – sort of dreamlike and mysterious – rows and rows of mountains, dead volcanoes with that strange greenish light on them. I paused a moment to gaze on it before I stepped out of the hut. "So, John Dolittle," I said to myself, "I suppose you are a big fool. But you chose to be a doctor when you were a youngster and this is the price you pay. You are a prisoner on this world for life. This landscape is what you will see for the remainder of your days. Well, what else could you do? So be it."

'I stepped over the door-sill into the open air.

Then I heard a cry from within the hut. The Moon Man, for the first time for days, was speaking to me. I turned and went back to his bedside.

'He was trying to sit up. "There, there," I said, "settle down and rest. I will come again tomorrow to see how you are." He sank back looking awfully feeble and I wondered whether I really ought to leave him. I felt his pulse again. It was good. Then suddenly he broke forth, speaking in a mixture of all sorts of languages, so that I had hard work keeping up with what he was trying to say.

' "My mind is sort of fuzzy," he whispered. "But I wanted to tell you that I know you have saved my life – without gaining anything for yourself. . . . While I was sleeping just now I seemed to remember something of the *days before there was a Moon*. I have not dealt with humans for so long. . . . But I remember – yes, I remember those times when I was on the Earth, ages and ages ago. I remember how humans acted towards one another. . . . You are what was called – er – a very true friend. Isn't that it, John Dolittle? . . . So I just wanted to tell you that any time you wish to return to your world I will help you in any way I can. . . . You are free to go – whenever you wish." '

The Doctor paused a moment.

'Well, you can imagine my astonishment. A moment before I had seen myself a prisoner on the Moon for life – giving up all hope of ever seeing the Earth, Puddleby, my friends, home, again. Now I was free. Suddenly all the unkind thoughts I had felt against this man fell away. I was bound to admit that he was greater, bigger, even than

I had guessed. Something in his recollections of
the Earth had made up his mind to this deter-
mination. And my coming to his assistance, the
very thing that should have ruined my chances of
ever getting home, had acted for me just the other
way. I was free!

'And then all at once I realized that, child as he
was, the Moon Man had wanted my company as
well as my help as a doctor. For some moments
I did not answer him. I was thinking – thinking
how much it meant to him to say those words,
"You are free to go." He was giving up the only
human friendship he had known in thousands of
years. And that is why, for a little, I did not speak.

'At last I said, "No one can know how long you
will live – probably for many thousands of years
yet, if you do as I tell you. When I return to the
Earth I mean to write a book, a book about the
Moon – and it's about you too, a great part of it.
People on the Earth, you know, have always
spoken of the *Man in the Moon*, but I hope that
when my book is written – and read – they will
come to speak of the *Gentleman in the Moon*.
Certainly I shall do my best to show them that
what I found in you, Otho Bludge, was not only
a great man but one of the truest gentlemen I
have ever known."

'Then I left him and went back to my camp.

'There is little more to tell. The next time I
visited him he was able to get up and move about.
He was as good as his word. He wasted no time
in preparing the bonfire for my smoke signal. For
this he got thousands and thousands of birds to
help him. They all brought a stick or twig of that

explosive wood which he had used for his own
signal. It reminded me of the time when I got the
birds in Africa to build the island in the lake out
of stones. But, for these creatures in the Moon to
gather together a bonfire whose smoke would be
large enough to be seen from the Earth, was a
tremendous undertaking.

'Just about the time it was finished I happened
to discover – in some astronomical almanacs
I had with me – that we were due to have
an eclipse in about ten days from then. This
interested me very much. For one thing I was
most keen to see an eclipse from the Moon and to
find out what the other planets looked like when
they came out in daylight hours. And, for another
thing, I felt sure that my signals would show
better when the Moon was partly in shadow.

'So I asked Otho to put off firing the bonfire till
the eclipse was under way. He became very
interested in the matter himself. He wanted to
know just how I had calculated that it would come
at a certain hour on a certain date. He suggested
that we should have two bonfires ready and set
them off separately – to make surer that one at
least of them would be seen. I found out, Stubbins,
also that when he tried to get a signal down to us
here, to tell us of the coming of the moth, he had
set off several before we happened to be looking
at the Moon and saw one.

'Then came the question of what sort of creature
I should have to fly me down. I had grown so big
by then; and there was considerable weight too in
the baggage which I wanted to bring with me.
The Giant Moth when we tried out a practice

flight could hardly rise from the ground under the load. So something else had to be found to make the trip.

'Birds were out of the question. Here we always think of birds as being larger than insects; but up there they were smaller – difference in diet again, I suppose. And then birds need more air – they have a different sort of breathing apparatus. The trip between the Moon and the Earth requires a tremendous amount of effort – very hard work. Getting through the dead belt, where there is practically no air at all, is easier for the insect fliers than any other. I doubt if a bird, no matter what his wing-spread, could manage it.

'Well, after a few experiments Otho and I decided to try the Mammoth Locust. You all saw what a tremendous creature he is. His way of flying is quite extraordinary – not at all the same as his cousins, the grasshopper, the cicada and the mantis. The locust flies both like a bird *and* an insect. The number of wing-beats per second is sort of betwixt and between. I have notes on that too.

'Anyway, we got the baggage and ourselves aboard this Mammoth Locust and made a trial flight. He could lift the load quite easily – that is, he could in that gravity. Whether he could have done the same with the Earth's gravity, I cannot say. But that didn't matter so much. When he got near to this world he would be coming *down*; and going back he would have no load to carry, beyond the weight of his own body.'

# Chapter Five
## THE FAREWELL

'WHEN the time was at hand for the eclipse to begin there was quite a gathering to see the show. I had calculated the exact point on the Moon — pretty exact, anyhow — from which it could best be seen. As I gazed over the great crowd it seemed as though every creature in the Moon had collected there. Of course this was not true. But it looked like it. I have never seen such a tremendous herd — not even when we called the animals together on the Island of No Man's Land off the coast of Africa to set up the Post Office and the classes in animal writing.

'But the crowd had not only come to see the eclipse; they had come to see me off. Many — some of them grateful patients whom I had cured of sicknesses — brought presents. Foodstuffs and the like. They wanted to show their gratitude. It was very touching. I thanked them as best I could, bade them goodbye and wished them luck. The Moon Man himself had said he would set off the bonfire signals. It was a ticklish business, this lighting of so much explosive stuff; and he was

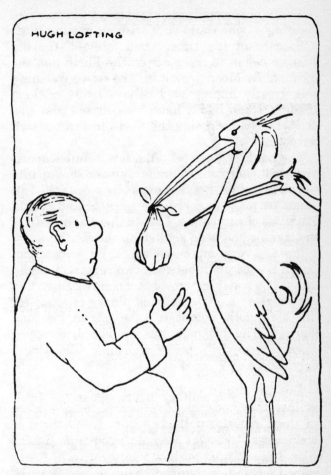

'Grateful patients brought presents – foodstuffs and the like'

the only one — with his big strides and speed of running — who could do it without getting hurt.

'Exactly at the time I had foretold, the big shadow began to creep across the Earth and the light on the Moon grew dim. The crowd watching was greatly impressed. I believe many of them thought I had had a hand in it myself and was deliberately darkening the Earth to suit my own purposes.

'The bonfires were set off, a few minutes apart, and great enormous columns of smoke shot up into the air. The fumes of that explosive wood rolled all about us making every one splutter and cough. Finally it cleared away. I hoped that one at least of the signals had been sighted on the Earth.

'It was a very impressive scene. We were standing in a wide plain between two ranges of mountains. The watching crowd of moon creatures had drawn away a little, leaving plenty of space for the Mammoth Locust to take off on his long journey. The baggage was on board, strapped down securely by ropes of vine-bark. Chee-Chee, Polynesia and I stood at the locust's side ready to go.

'Suddenly one solitary figure separated itself from the ring of watchers and stalked out into the open towards me. It was a cat.'

Polynesia jumped as usual, and Jip snorted something between a growl and a grunt.

'She came stalking across the wide open space all alone. When she got to me she said, "Doctor Dolittle, I want to go with you." That was all. I had never been fond of cats. And yet I know of no exact reason why I should feel less friendly towards her kind than I did towards any other sort of animal. On the other hand, I knew of course that if I took her into my household down here many of you would object.

'I argued with her. I told her cats had many enemies in the world where I was going. She said, "Don't bother about my enemies, Doctor. I'll take care of them." Then – still hoping to discourage her, I said, "But you understand that if I take you, there is to be no killing – birds, mice and so forth. We can't have any of that, you know." All she answered was, "John Dolittle, I'm a moon cat. For thousands of years we have not killed birds – or any living creature. We have learned here to live on other things. We hunt no more. I want to see the Earth, where my people came from. Take me with you."

'Well – there you are – there was no answering her argument. She was running a big risk. And she knew it.

' "Very well," I said at last. "Get aboard the locust." And without another word she climbed up on to the insect's back. There Chee-Chee stowed her in a crate and made her fast for the big journey.

'But the worst part of the whole business for me was saying goodbye to Otho Bludge. It was not easy. As I told you, I had realized of a sudden how terribly lonely the poor fellow was going to be. Perhaps he would never have felt so if I had not come to the Moon. It is true this was his own doing – yet, so far as his losing my company was concerned, it made no matter. He had said very little to me after he had told me I could go. But now when he came striding over towards us, as we stood by the locust's side, I wondered what was going on inside his mind. He was about to say goodbye to the first human being he had talked with in thousands of years.

'He held out his hand. I remember asking myself how it was he had not forgotten that this was the fashion in which the people of the Earth bade one another farewell. I did not know what to say. At last it was he who spoke.

' "Goodbye," he said, in an awkward kind of way. "Do you think that – some day – you may come back?"

'Oh,' quacked Dab-Dab, 'I do hope you didn't promise him you would, Doctor!'

'No,' said John Dolittle, 'I didn't promise anything. Although I must admit the Moon was a most interesting place to visit. No – I just said, "Well, Otho, keep off the goy-goy and you'll still live longer than any of us. I have left a dozen bottles of the medicine in your hut. But you won't need them if you will only follow the diet I have told you to."

'It was a terrible moment. I was anxious to get it over with. He turned and moved away. Evidently at the very last he would sooner not see our going. I climbed aboard the locust. My size, you must remember, was terrific. But even when I lay down flat on the creature's back – over his thorax, his shoulders – there still seemed to be lots of room to spare. We had on board many of those oxygen lilies, Stubbins, which we used on the other trip. I pulled one up, handy to dip my nose in. The locust scrabbled his feet in the sand of the valley so he could make a good take-off. "Goodbye!" yelled the crowd. "Goodbye!" we called back. With a terrific kick of his hind legs the insect shot up into the air and spread his wings.

'The trip was terrible. I suppose having stayed on the Moon so long my lungs had got sort of accustomed to the air up there and unaccustomed to the air of the Earth — to say nothing of the dreadful dead belt. Anyway, when we did reach that terrible part of the journey I honestly thought it was all over with me. The locust had got instructions about the navigation from Jamara Bumblelily, the Giant Moth, before he set off. But it was terrible anyhow. I grabbed one of the oxygen flowers and stuck my face in it. Nevertheless I became unconscious — and stayed so till after we landed. When I came to at last I heard you, Stubbins, talking with Polynesia. Everything was still. I looked up at the Moon, steady in the sky. Last time I had seen it, it was swinging around the heavens like a crazy thing.

'Well, that's all. Here I am, none the worse for the trip — the most interesting journey I have ever made in my life.'

Quite clearly the Doctor felt that his tale had rather saddened us towards the end. As a matter of fact all the animals were certainly very serious when he finished.

'Tell me, Doctor,' said Jip at last, 'do you think the Moon Man will be able to manage by himself now?'

'Of course he will,' Dab-Dab broke in. 'How did he manage before the Doctor went there?'

'I wasn't asking you, Dab-Dab,' said Jip quietly. I was asking the Doctor.'

'Oh, I think he'll be all right,' said John Dolittle after a pause.

'He'll miss you, won't he?' said Jip. 'Mighty sporting of him to let you go, wasn't it? – Humph! The "Gentleman in the Moon". Good luck to him!'

'Poor man!' said Whitey – always sentimental and romantic. 'Left all alone!'

'Hum! Hum!' said Gub-Gub. 'It must be kind of hard to be the only one of your kind in a world.'

'But you won't go back, Doctor, will you?' said Dab-Dab anxiously. 'After all, you've seen the Moon now – spring, summer, autumn and winter. There's no sense in your fooling with it any more, is there? You know what I mean?'

'Yes, I understand, Dab-Dab.' said the Doctor. 'But' – his voice trailed off in a sleepy tone – 'it was – er – well, it *was* a very interesting place.'

I saw that he was getting tired. I made a signal to the animals and Matthew. They understood.

'All right, Doctor,' I said. 'Thank you. We will now leave you in peace to sleep. Good night!'

I folded up my notebooks. John Dolittle's head was nodding on his chest. We all crept out on tiptoe and closed the door behind us.

# Chapter Six
## SETTING THE ZOO TO RIGHTS

IT was not until almost the end of the summer that the Doctor got back to his ordinary size. He was now no longer afraid of being seen; and he moved about the house without upsetting things or smashing furniture; and he was very happy about it.

First of all he went over the whole garden from end to end. Though I had done the best I could to keep it up in good condition for him, there was much of course that his eye fell on which mine had overlooked. John Dolittle was a very good gardener himself and very particular. (Dab-Dab always used to say he never seemed to mind how untidy his house was, as long as the garden was spick and span.) Gub-Gub and I – and sometimes Matthew when he was about – helped him with the work; dividing up the iris roots; pegging down the raspberry canes; digging up and re-sowing some of the turf patches that had grown bare and brown.

'The coming of autumn, Stubbins,' said he, 'is always the most important season for a sensible gardener. That's the time when we put the earth to bed, as it were. If you get the ground and your plants and trees in good condition for their long winter sleep, you will have something to show in the spring.'

When we came to look over the big enclosure which we had called the zoo the emptiness of it seemed to sadden him. He gazed over the long walled-in lawn some moments without speaking; but I knew what was in his mind. So did Jip.

'Humph!' muttered the Doctor after a while, 'those dog-houses down at the bottom look pretty sad, don't they? The roofs all full of holes and rotten. We must do something to clean up this mess, Stubbins. A year seems such a short time, and yet what a lot can happen in it!'

'Look here, Doctor,' said Jip, 'why can't we repair them and start the Home for Cross-bred Dogs over again? There's a half-breed setter down in the town. His name is Flip. He has no home at all. He gets his meals from any old place – off rubbish heaps mostly. And there are a lot of other dogs too. Couldn't we take them in, the same as we used to when you kept open house for stray dogs?'

'Well, Jip, I'd love to,' said the Doctor. 'They surely were jolly times when we had the dogs' home running full blast. You remember that little rascal, Quetch, the Scotty who used to run the dogs' gymnasium for us – and bossed you all over the place when we had the jumping contests? And wasn't that a wonderful yarn – when he told us the story of his life? My, what a character he was! But you see, Jip, I don't know about the money side of it. A lot of dogs need a lot of food.

It seems to me I've got to live off Stubbins' salary
here — of three shillings and sixpence a week —
till I begin to make something from my new book.'

'Well, but, Doctor,' said Jip. 'Why can't we take
in just Flip for the present — till you're feeling
richer? I'm afraid he'll get shot one of these days
for stealing people's chickens or something. No
one takes care of him. He's just a tramp. He comes
round to the front gate twice a week to see if I
have any old bones to give him. Most of the time
he's practically starving.'

'Humph! Starving, eh?' said the Doctor seriously.
He looked at me. 'Can we manage it, do you think,
Stubbins?'

'Oh, surely, Doctor,' said I. 'We'll manage
somehow. We always seem to have milk and
vegetables, any way.'

'Good!' said the Doctor. 'Milk and vegetables are
much better for a dog than a lot of meat. All right,
Jip, bring your friend in next time he calls and
we'll fix up one of the dog-houses for him here.'

The white mouse, always inquisitive, had been
following us around on the inspection of the
garden. He now piped up in his funny squeaky
little voice.

'Oh, and Doctor, wouldn't it be a good idea if we
set up the Rat and Mouse Club again too? There's
a new family of mice up in the attic. And you
know Dab-Dab would much sooner have them out
of the house, down here instead. It won't be any
trouble. I can fix up our old Rat Town just as it
was. I know how they like it, you see. And they'll
be no expense. A few crusts of bread and rinds of
cheese. It would be lots of fun to have them here

once more, don't you think? Then we could have
them telling us stories over the kitchen fire after
supper — just like old times. Do let's start the Rat
and Mouse Club again!'

'Humph!' said the Doctor thoughtfully. 'I don't
see why not. It would make the place more home-
like. I certainly hate to see the zoo enclosure all
empty and deserted like this. Yes, let's set up the
Rat and Mouse Club. I'll leave the matter in your
hands, Whitey. At least we can afford that.'

And then the old lame horse who had been helping us weed the garden with a cultivator put in
his say.

'Doctor,' he said, 'how about the Retired Cab
and Wagon Horses' Association — you know
the farm you bought for them about two miles
away?'

'Ah, yes,' said the Doctor, 'to be sure, to be sure.
I'd forgotten all about them. Tell me, how are
they getting on?'

'Well,' said the old fellow, swishing the flies off
with his tail, 'I hear there have not been any new
members joined of late. But the fences need
repairing. Dogs getting in and yapping and snap-
ping about the place — in spite of all the signs we
put up, "Trespassers Will Be Prosecuted — Dogs
Will Be Kicked," you remember?'

'Yes, yes, of course,' said the Doctor.

'And the scratching-post you set for them — it
got pushed down. And they would like another.'

'Dear me, dear me,' said John Dolittle. 'Yes, I
remember how they used to like to scratch their
necks — on the top of the hill there, where they
could see the view as the Sun went down. Well,

I'll certainly have to attend to that. I'll go over
with you in the morning and see about it.'

And so it was that before very long most of the
old institutions which the Doctor had set up for
the comfort and happiness of animals got put
back into running order after his long stay on the
Moon. All of his own animal household were very
happy about this – and, I was surprised to find,
Dab-Dab in particular.

'Tommy,' she said to me one evening, 'this is a
good thing. It will keep John Dolittle out of
mischief – I mean keep him away from his book
for a while more anyhow. Why shouldn't he have
a good time giving the animals a good time? So
long as he doesn't start any of those crazy
charitable ideas for pests, like the Country House
for House Flies. Poof!' (She shrugged up her wings
in disgust.) 'Don't let him start *that* again. He'll
have a Wardrobe for Clothes Moths or a Bedroom
for Bed-bugs before you know where you are.'

# Chapter Seven
## SQUIB THE COCKER SPANIEL

**B**UT these departments of his big establishment were not the only things that began leading John Dolittle back into his old ways of living. In former days the most important concern in 'the little house with the big garden' had been the dispensary, where animals and creatures of all sorts came to him for the treatment of their sickness and injuries. Of course any one can understand that as soon as he began to move about and let himself be seen word would get abroad to the animals outside that the famous man was back in Puddleby once more.

And, sure enough, it was only a few weeks later that our patients began to call — first a pair of rabbits, very scared and timid. I found them on the doorstep at the crack of dawn one morning. Could they see the Doctor, please? I asked them what was the matter. They said they had a sick baby — didn't know what was the trouble with it. I told them the Doctor was still in bed and I didn't like to wake him because he was very tired. Where was the baby?

'Oh,' said the mother rabbit, almost bursting

into tears, 'it's not far away. If you'll come with
us we'll show you and maybe if you bring it back
here the Doctor will be awake by then. But we
must make haste. It's very sick.'

'All right,' I said, 'I'll come with you. Lead the
way.'

Well, the mother rabbit was in a hurry. She and
her mate shot out the garden gate and went
bolting down the road like a streak of lightning.
Time and again I had to call to them to wait and
let me catch up. After they had gone about a mile
towards Oxenthorpe they left the highway and
started off across country. Over ditches, ploughed
fields and swamps they led me – under hedges,
through copses, over hill and dale. At last they
came to a stop before a hole in a bank beside a
wood.

'The baby's down there,' said the mother.
'Please hurry up and get it out. It's terribly ill.'

Of course there was no earthly chance of my
getting down a hole that size. But there was a
farm nearby. I ran over to it. It was still very
early in the morning and no one was about. I
found a garden spade in a turnip field. I borrowed
it and ran back to the rabbits. Then I got the
father to show me about how far his hole ran into
the bank. I dug down in that spot and got the
young one out. He certainly looked pretty ill –
breathing very hard. Some sort of asthma I
suspected. I picked him up, left the spade where
the farmer would find it, and started off, on the
run, back to the Doctor's house with both the
parents at my heels.

John Dolittle was up and shaving by the time

we got there. He gave one look at the baby rabbit, dropped his razor, took the patient out of my hands and ran down the stairs with it to the dispensary. There he swabbed its throat out with some kind of disinfectant and laid it in a shoe-box on a bed of hay.

'You only just caught it in time, Stubbins,' he said. 'I think it will mend all right. But we'll have to keep an eye on it for a few days. Put it up in my bedroom — under the bed. Tell the parents they can live there too for a few days. Give them some apples. Hah, it's a fine youngster! We'll fix it up all right.'

At breakfast I told Dab-Dab about it. She rolled her eyes towards the ceiling with a sigh.

'We'll have to take the carpet up.' she said. 'There will be apple-cores all over the room. Ah, well! We might have expected it. That's the way it always begins — after he's been away. Now we'll have every kind of animal in the countryside calling on him with their toothaches and bruises and blisters!'

And, sure enough, she was right. From that time on the animal patients began to arrive thick and fast, at all hours of the day and night. Foxes, badgers, otters, squirrels, weasels, hedgehogs, moles, rats, mice and every kind of bird, formed a line ouside the dispensary door — a line which seemed to grow for ever longer and longer. The wild animals' world had learned that the great doctor was back.

And so the little house suddenly became a very busy place. The Doctor was here, there and everywhere. Jip's friend Flip came and was given a

' "The baby's down there," said the mother. "Please hurry!" '

comfortable home in one of the dog-houses in the
zoo enclosure. In fact he found it so comfortable,
and enjoyed being a guest of the Doctor's so much,
that next time he visited the town he told all his
friends about it. And as soon as it got abroad in
dog society that the famous Home for Cross-bred
Dogs was open once more, we had all descriptions
of waifs and strays and mongrels for miles around
wagging their tails at the gates and asking to be
taken in as members. The Doctor never could
resist a hard-luck story from animals. And we
soon had a wonderful collection down there in the
zoo enclosure. Never had I seen such mixtures —
crosses between greyhounds and dachshunds,
between Airedales and mastiffs, Irish terriers and
foxhounds. But the more mixed they were the
better the Doctor seemed to like them.

'They're always more intelligent and interesting, these cross-breds, Stubbins,' he said, 'than
the pedigree dogs. This is splendid. I always like
to have lots of dogs around.'

He *did* have them; there was no question about
that. The real trouble came when not only the
stray dogs of the neighbourhood — those who had
no owners or places to go at night — but the
regular dogs, many of them thoroughbreds, heard
of the 'Home' in the Doctor's garden and just ran
away and came to us.

This, as can be easily understood, caused a lot
of trouble for John Dolittle. (It had done the same
before, as a matter of fact.) Angry owners of pet
poodles, dogs who had won prizes and blue
ribbons in shows, came round to see the Doctor.
Furiously they accused him of luring away their

precious darlings from their proper homes. And
the Doctor had hard work pacifying them. One
case I remember that amused me very much. It
was a Cocker spaniel. When she arrived at the
house she told the Doctor she was annoyed with
her owner because she would treat her as a lap-
dog.

'And you know, Doctor,' she said very haughtily,
'we Cockers are *not* lap-dogs, like the King
Charles or Pekinese spaniels — those piffling
fleabags who do nothing but sit on cushions. *We*
are not that kind. We are sporting dogs. I can't
stand my owner. I wish to live my own life. We're
descended from the water spaniels — a very old
and respected breed.'

'Of course, of course,' said the Doctor. 'I quite
understand.'

'I don't want to sit on sofas,' the dog went on.
'I want to run in the woods — to smell the deer.
I love going after deer. I've never caught one and
I don't suppose I'd know what to do with it if I did.
But it's the fun of the thing, don't you see? My
mistress says I mustn't get myself wet, running
through the long grass and all that. But I just
hate the life of drawing-rooms and afternoon teas!
I want to come and live with you and all those
jolly mongrels down in your zoo.'

'I see, I see,' said the Doctor. 'And I quite understand your point of view. Quite, quite. But what
am I to say to your owner when she traces you
back here and comes to tell me I've stolen her
dog?'

'Oh, let her go and buy herself a toy one,' said the
spaniel, 'one of those made out of rags. It would

do just as well for her. She doesn't know anything about real dogs.'

Well, that was the kind of thing the Doctor found himself faced with all the time. And it certainly kept him busy. This particular spaniel did actually stay with us. We called her Squib; but, as the Doctor had prophesied, her owner, a very elegant lady of one of the county's best families, called and started a rumpus. However, Squib was so rude and unfriendly to her former mistress and made such a fuss about being taken away, that the lady, after the Doctor had explained things to her, finally went off and left her with us. And the spaniel to her great delight was allowed to join the Home for Cross-bred Dogs.

Although she was frightfully well-bred, a champion in her class and all that, she never boasted about her pedigree to the other dogs. Squib's one great ambition was to trail a deer and run him down in the woods. She never succeeded – with the short legs she had. But it didn't matter anyway. In fact it was just as well she never did. Always she had still something to look forward to. As she had explained to the Doctor, the fun of the game was the thing that counted.

# Chapter Eight
## HOW TO GET INTO JAIL?

OF course as time went on the Doctor became more and more anxious to get at his notes and the writing of his book about the Moon. One evening, after all our work for the day had been attended to, we were sitting in the kitchen. Matthew Mugg, the cats'-meat-man, was with us. It was nearly midnight and I had packed all the animals off to bed because both John Dolittle and myself were pretty tired.

The Doctor was filling his pipe from the big tobacco-jar, and when he got it lighted and going well he said to me, 'You know, Stubbins, I can't see how I'll ever get that book started, as things are going at present.'

'Yes, Doctor,' I said, 'I know what you mean.'

'It isn't that I begrudge the time I give to the animals here, you understand,' he went on. 'It's just that there *are* only twenty-four hours to the day. And no matter how I try to arrange it, I don't – I simply don't – seem to find any time for writing. You see, I always feel that these animals that call upon me with their troubles, well, that is a living, an immediate, thing. The book should be able to wait. Maybe nobody will take any notice of it, anyway, when it comes out. But I do want to get it written. I *hope* it's going to be a very important work.'

'You ought to go away somewhere, Doctor,' said the cats'-meat-man — 'so you could 'ave peace and quiet. From what Tommy tells me, you ain't likely to get none 'ere.'

'That's an idea,' cried John Dolittle. 'To go away — but where?'

'Take a seaside 'oliday, Doctor,' said Matthew. 'Go down to Margate. Lovely place! I got a cousin down there in the lobster-fishin' business. Nobody would bother you in Margate. It's far enough off from Puddleby so not even the animals 'ereabouts would know where you'd gone.'

The Doctor frowned slightly as he looked into the bowl of his pipe.

'Yes,' he said, 'but you see, Matthew, there's always that wretched question of money. Where can a man go without money?'

Matthew drummed a moment on the table with his fingers.

'Now, Doctor,' he said presently, 'the main thing you're lookin' for is peace and quiet, ain't it?'

'That's it,' said John Dolittle. 'A place where I can write my book undisturbed.'

'Well,' said Matthew. 'There's only one place I know where a man can get all the peace and quiet 'e wants and it don't cost 'im nothin'.'

'Where's that?' asked the Doctor.

'In jail,' said Matthew.

'Oh,' said the Doctor, a little surprised. 'Ah, yes, I see. I hadn't thought of that. Yet — er — after

all, it *is* an idea. Quite an idea. But tell me – er
– how does one go about getting into jail?'

'That's a fine thing for you to be askin' *me*, John
Dolittle! My trouble wasn't never 'ow to get into
jail; it was always 'ow to stay out of it.'

Both the Doctor and I knew Matthew's occa-
sional troubles with the police. His great
weakness was poaching, that is, snaring rabbits
and pheasants on other people's property.
Nothing on earth could ever persuade him this
was wrong. And whenever he was missing and
suddenly turned up again after several weeks'
absence the Doctor never asked him where he had
been. For he guessed he most likely had had one
of his 'little run-ins with the police' as he called
them. But tonight neither of us could keep from
laughing outright.

'Now listen,' said Matthew, leaning forward,
'let's go into committee on this. First thing we got
to decide is which jail we got to get you into, see?
There's lots o' difference in 'em. I wouldn't recom-
mend you Puddleby jail. No – too draughty. I got
an awful nooralgy in me face last time I was
there. Well, then, there's Oxenthorpe jail. No –
come to think of it – I wouldn't pick that one
neither. It's a nice jail, you understand. But the
old Justice of the Peace what sits on the bench up
there is a snooty old bloke and 'e's liable to give
you 'ard.'

'Hard?' said the Doctor. 'I don't quite understand.'

' 'Ard labour,' said Matthew. 'You know, work.
You 'ave to work all the time you're in there –
makin' ropes and that kind o' thing. You wouldn't
want that. You want peace and quiet so you can

write a book. No, Oxenthorpe is out. But then there's Gilesborough. Ah, now that's the place you—'

'But excuse me,' the Doctor put in. 'One has to do something to get into jail, doesn't one? I mean, you must commit some sort of an offence, break the law. What?'

'Oh, that's easy, Doctor,' said the cats'-meat-man. 'Listen, all you got to do is go up to a policeman and push 'im in the face. You'll get into jail all right.'

'Er — er — well, now wait a minute,' said the Doctor. 'I'm not what's called conventional, as you know, Matthew. In fact, I too have been in prison. I was thrown into a dungeon in Africa by Prince Bumpo's father, the King of the Jolliginki. But I didn't have to do anything for that. The King just didn't like strangers. And I can't say that I blame him — seeing what his experience with them had been. But, to come back: I think that your idea sounds good in many ways. A prison, with high stone walls, should be a splendid place to write.'

'The grub's rotten — that's the only thing,' said Matthew, reaching for the tobacco-jar.

'Well, that won't bother me,' said John Dolittle. 'I'm eating as little as possible now, you know, on account of my weight. But the way to get into jail is the thing that may prove difficult. Listen, Matthew: don't you think I could do something less violent? I mean, instead of pushing a policeman's face, couldn't I just — er — break a window or something?'

'Oh, positively,' said Matthew. 'There's lots of ways of getting into jail. But, you see, just for bustin' a window you'd only get a sentence of a few days. 'Ow long was you thinkin' you'd want to stay?'

'Er – I just don't know, Matthew,' said the Doctor. 'But certainly until I get most of my book finished.'

'Well,' said the cats'-meat-man, 'there's no need to worry about that yet a while. If the judge only gives you fourteen days and you want to stay longer, all you got to do is tear up your bed or something like that. Or, if they puts you out, you can just break another window and come back in again, see? That part's easy. Now I got to be goin'. Theodosia always gets kind of fussy if I'm out late at night. But you think it over, Doctor. If you wants peace and quiet there's no place like a prison cell. But when you starts your window-breakin' you better let me come and 'elp you. No, don't thank me, Doctor, it'll be a pleasure, I assure you! 'Twould never do to 'ave no bunglin'. The job's got to be done right. Yer might get into trouble! And choose Gilesborough. Trust me. It's a nice jail. Good night!'

# Chapter Nine
## GILESBOROUGH

AFTER Matthew had left, the Doctor and I sat on chatting for a while longer. It was quite plain, as John Dolittle talked, that he was becoming more and more taken up with the idea of jail as his one best place to go for finishing his book. The work at his house interested him no end, but there was clearly no possible chance of his getting at his writing while he stayed at home. He felt that this book was a greater thing than he had done, or ever would do. At the same time he hated to leave his patients. He put these matters before me now for consideration and I was very flattered that he wanted my opinion.

'Well, Doctor,' I said, 'it seems to me that it is a question of which is the most important, the book or the patients.'

'Quite so, Stubbins,' said he. 'That's just it. And it's hard for me to make up my mind. You see, as I told you, so many of these sick animals have come to rely on me – and me alone – to help them in their troubles.'

'Yes, but just the same,' I said, 'how did they get

along while you were away before? I can't see why
you feel you must take care of everybody and
everything in the world, Doctor. That's more than
any one could do. It won't take you for ever to
write your book. Why can't the patients manage
without your help for that length of time, the
same as they did while you were away in the
Moon?'

He shrugged his shoulders but did not answer.

The next day I talked the matter over with
Dab-Dab.

'Tommy,' said she, 'that man Matthew Mugg is
a scallywag, but he's got brains. Jail may not be
the pleasantest place in the world. But don't you
see what's going to happen if John Dolittle doesn't
go away somewhere?'

'What?' I asked.

'He'll try and do both things,' said Dab-Dab.
'He'll try to look after all these blessed animals
– many of them aren't really sick, you know, they
just want to get a look at the great man and then
go back and brag about it to their friends – *and*
he'll try to write the book. Both at the same time.
He'll get ill from overwork. No, the more I think
of it, the surer I feel. Matthew's right. The place
for John Dolittle is jail. He'll be safe there.'

Well, it was towards the end of that week that
the Doctor came to a decision. We had a very long
line of patients calling on him – worse than
usual. The cases were not serious ones, but they
kept him on the go from the time he got out of bed
till the time he went back to it – long after midnight. To make matters worse still, four new dogs
arrived who wished to become members of the

'Home.' And the same afternoon Whitey discovered two new families of wild mice who said
they'd like to join the Rat and Mouse Club. When
I went with the Doctor up to his bedroom that
night he was all worn out.

'Stubbins,' he said, as he sank into a chair, 'it's
no use my staying here any longer. I've just got
to go away.'

'Yes, Doctor,' I said, 'I think you're right.'

'Tomorrow, Stubbins,' said he, 'we'll go over to
Gilesborough. You get hold of Matthew for me.
I am a little bit afraid of what he may do. But,
on the other hand, I am not – er – as experienced
as he is in these matters. So I think it would
be a good idea if we had him with us, don't
you?'

'Yes,' I said, 'I do.'

'Anyway,' he went on, 'call me early, won't you?
We must get those notes arranged. I fancy one is
not allowed to take much baggage when one goes
to jail. We'll have to copy the notes out on to
ordinary paper, you know – much less bulky than
those palm-leaf sheets I brought down from the
Moon.'

'Very good,' said I. 'We can manage that all
right. Now get some sleep, Doctor. It's a quarter
to one.'

I was down very early the next morning and,
thinking I was up ahead of everybody, I was tip-
toeing through the house on my way out to visit
Matthew when I found the whole family sitting at
breakfast round the kitchen-table.

'Well, Dab-Dab,' I said, 'he's going!'

'Who's going?' asked Gub-Gub.

'The Doctor,' I said.

'Where is he going?' asked the white mouse.

'To jail,' I answered.

'Why is he going?' asked Jip.

'Because he has to,' said I, as patiently as I could.

'When is he going?' asked Too-Too.

'As soon as he can,' I said.

It was the usual bombardment of questions that I got regularly whenever I broke any news of the Doctor.

'Now look here,' said Dab-Dab, addressing the rest of them. 'Stop bothering Tommy with your chatter. The Doctor has decided to go to jail so he can be free.'

'Free — in jail!' cried the white mouse.

'Just that,' said Dab-Dab. 'He needs quiet. And you must all understand that where he is going is to be kept a secret.'

'Dear me!' sighed the white mouse. 'We always seem to be having to keep secrets round here.'

'Well, there's to be no *seeming* about this,' snorted Dab-Dab. 'No one is to know where John Dolittle is going. Is that clear to all of you? For a while the Doctor has just got to disappear from the world — the world of animals as well as of people. All of us must see to it that no one, absolutely no one, gets to hear of where he has gone.'

After a glass of milk I hurried away to see Matthew. The cats'-meat-man agreed to meet us, the Doctor and myself, in Gilesborough that afternoon.

On my return I got the notes arranged as the

Doctor wanted. We did not plan to take them all
with us at once. We felt sure I could bring him
more later, as he needed them. And so it was only
with a satchel for baggage that we set out
together to walk to Gilesborough – a distance of
some seven miles from Puddleby.

I must confess that I had to smile to myself as
we set off. John Dolittle, the great traveller who
had undertaken such adventurous voyages, was
starting off on the strangest journey of all: to go
to jail! And for the first time in his life he was
worried that he might not get there.

Gilesborough was quite a place – in many ways
more important than Puddleby. It was a Saxon
town, the centre of a 'hundred,' as it was called in
the old days. Its square-towered little church sat
up among its surrounding oak trees and could be
seen from a long way off. What is more, it was a
market-town. Every Friday fine cattle were
driven in – Jersey cows, sheep, and Berkshire
pigs – by the farmers of the neighbourhood. And
then once a year, just before Michaelmas, there
was the Goose Fair. This was attended by visitors
for many miles around and was a county-wide
affair of great importance.

I had visited the town before; and I had enjoyed
seeing those jolly farmers with their apple-
cheeked wives gathering in the White Hart Inn
or the Fitz-Hugh Arms Hotel to talk over the fine
points of the sheep shown in the market pens, or
neighbours' calves sold at new high prices. They
always had splendid horses for their gigs, these
men, in which they drove to town – even if the
gigs were in sad need of repairs, painting and

washing. Taken all in all, Gilesborough was one of the spots of Old England any one would love to visit.

The Doctor and I arrived there on a late Friday afternoon. The market was over and the farmers had retired to take their last mug of cider at the taverns before going home. We found the cats'-meat-man at our meeting-place, waiting for us.

'Now look here, Matthew,' said the Doctor, 'about this window-breaking business: you understand I wouldn't want to break the windows of any poor people – those who couldn't afford it, you know.'

'A worthy thought,' said Matthew, 'a werry worthy thought. I take it you'd like better to break the windows of the wealthy. So would I. Well, 'ow about the bank – the Gilesborough Investment Corporation? They've got lots of money and they'd be sure to prosecute, too, mind yer. That's important. They just loves to prosecute people. Yes, Doctor, that's the idea. Let's bust the bank's winders. They're made of plate glass – lovely! They'll be closed to customers now, but the clerks and cashiers will still be there. We'll go and take a whack at the bank – helegant! Now, let me see – where are some good stones? Yes – 'ere we are! You take a couple in your pockets and I'll take a few too. Wouldn't never do to 'ave no bunglin'!'

Matthew picked up a handful of large pebbles from the roadway. He handed some to the Doctor and put some more in his own pockets.

'Now,' said he, 'we just go and stroll down the

street — saunterin' like. Then when we gets in front of the bank we—'

'Just a minute,' said the Doctor. 'Are you going to throw the stone to break the window, or am I?'

'It just depends, Doctor,' said Matthew, 'on how much of a crowd we finds in front of the bank and the distribution of the population, as you might say, see?'

'No, I can't say that I see — quite,' said the Doctor.

'Well,' said the cats'-meat-man, 'you got to use judgement in these things — tactics, yer know. You might find a whole lot of people in between you and the bank front, and you wouldn't be able to let fly proper, while me — I might see a chance when you wouldn't, see? It won't do to 'ave no bunglin'! You take your cue from me, Doctor. I'll get you into jail all right!'

Matthew went ahead of us a little. The Doctor, with me following behind, was clearly worried.

'I don't quite like this, Stubbins,' he whispered. 'But I suppose Matthew knows what he's doing.'

'I hope so, Doctor,' I said.

We arrived in front of the bank. It was in a wide square known as the Bargate. Many people were on the pavements. The Doctor was craning his neck here and there, dodging about, trying to see over their heads. Suddenly there was a crash, followed by the noise of falling glass;

'It sounds to me,' said the Doctor, 'as though Matthew has been helping us.'

Before I had time to answer him I heard cries from the people around us: 'Stop him! Stop thief!

He tried to break into the bank. Stop him! Catch him!'

'Dear me!' said the Doctor. 'Is it Matthew they're after?'

We saw a scuffle going on ahead of us.

'Yes — yes!' cried the Doctor. 'That's he. Matthew's broken the bank window. Follow me, Stubbins.'

We shouldered our way into the crowd that was now gathering thick and fast. In the centre of it, sure enough, we found Matthew struggling in the grasp of a policeman.

'Pardon me,' said the Doctor politely, touching the policeman on the shoulder, 'but it was I who threw the stone — er — thereby breaking the window.'

'I might believe you, sir,' said the policeman — 'being as how you *looks* an honest gent. But I seen him with my own eyes. Took a stone out of his pocket — with me right behind him, and threw it through the bank's front window. Besides, I know this cove. He's a poacher over from Puddleby way. A bad lot, he is. Come along o' me, young feller. And it's my duty to warn you that anything you say may be held agin you in court!'

And poor Matthew was marched away towards the jail.

'But, Constable,' said the Doctor to the policeman, 'you must listen to me. I–'

'Never mind,' whispered Matthew. 'Don't you come to the court, Doctor. You don't want to be known there — not yet. No cause to worry about me. I'll be out of that jail almost afore they puts me in there. I know all the locks, see. . . . Yes, I'm

'Matthew struggling in the grasp of a policeman'

a-comin', old funny-face. Stop pullin' – gimme a chance to talk to me friend before I goes to the scaffold, can't yer? I'm surprised at you!' (Matthew dropped his voice to a whisper again.) 'I'll be seein' yer, Doctor, Just a little mistake, see? If at first yer don't succeed, try, try – yer know the old sayin'. Better wait till I can 'elp yer. Wouldn't do to 'ave no bunglin', you know. I'll get yer into jail all right, never fear!'

# Chapter Ten
## LADY MATILDA BEAMISH

JOHN DOLITTLE was all for following our unlucky friend, but I persuaded him not to.

'I think he'll be all right, Doctor,' I said. 'And certainly, as he told you, you don't want to get known at the Court House yet – for fear they think there is something funny about us.'

'They'll think that in any case if we go on this way,' said the Doctor gloomily. 'But, Stubbins, I can't bear to feel I have got Matthew into jail. For years I've been trying to persuade him to keep out of it. I almost wish I hadn't started out on this crazy idea.'

'Oh, Doctor,' said I, 'as far as Matthew is concerned, I'm sure you have nothing to worry about. He's so – well – he's so experienced in these matters.'

'Yes,' said the Doctor thoughtfully, 'that is true. But still if I'm to get into Gilesborough jail I don't think I should wait for his assistance any further. I'd better leave the bank alone, don't you think?'

'Yes, Doctor,' said I. 'I think I would.'

We went on strolling down the main street till presently we came to the outskirts of the town, where there were no shops any more, just private houses.

'This looks like a prosperous place,' said the Doctor, stopping before a large house with a very elegant front. 'I should think the folks here could easily afford a broken window, what? Well, here goes! Now listen, Stubbins, you better keep out of the way. We don't want the wrong man arrested a second time.'

The Doctor drew a stone from his pocket and let fly at a big window on the ground floor. Another crash, and more sounds of falling glass. We waited, watching the front door for some one to come out. No one came. Presently an urchin stepped up behind us.

'Mister,' said he, 'there ain't no use in breaking the windows in that house.'

'Why?' asked the Doctor.

'The people's gone away,' said the boy. 'Yes, gone abroad for the winter. I broke all the windows in the back yesterday and no one even chased me off the place!'

'Good gracious!' murmured the Doctor. 'Have I got to spoil every house in this town before I get stopped? Come, Stubbins, let us go on.'

Once more we sauntered, looking for points of attack.

'I don't seem to be doing very well,' said the Doctor dismally. 'I had no idea how difficult it was to get into jail.'

'Well, Doctor,' I said, 'I suppose there's a good deal in looking the part, as they say. Matthew didn't seem to find it difficult to get into jail.'

'Look,' said the Doctor, pointing down the
street. 'There's another big house — with lots of
carriages driving up to the door. I wonder what's
going on there.'

'Most likely they're giving a tea-party, or
something of the kind,' I said. 'See, there's a
policeman there regulating the traffic.'

'A policeman!' cried the Doctor. 'Why, so there
is! This is splendid, Stubbins. I can't go wrong this
time. Important people with plenty of money; a
party going on; crowds of witnesses, *and* a
policeman. He'll just be bound to arrest me. I'll
report him for neglect of duty if he doesn't!'

When we came up to the house we saw there
was quite a gathering of townspeople watching
the guests driving up in their carriages. It certainly seemed to be quite a large and elegant
affair which was going on. The Doctor told me to
hang back; and he elbowed his way into the crowd
till he was near enough to make sure of his aim.
By standing on tiptoe, from where I was I could
see him and his tall hat plainly. Again he took a
stone from his pocket and scored a bull's-eye on
the largest of the ground-floor windows.

Another crash — and once more the clatter of
falling glass. This noise was instantly followed by
indignant cries from the crowd. Everybody drew
away from the Doctor as though they feared he
was dangerous. Suddenly, as it were, he was left
all by himself in the centre of a small ring,
blushing ridiculously but looking quite happy
and triumphant. The policeman came through
the crowd and looked at him. He was clearly very
puzzled by the respectable appearance of the

stone-thrower. His eye roamed over the Doctor's satchel, his top hat, and his kind, genial face.

'Pardon me, sir,' said he, 'but was it you who threw that stone?'

'Yes,' said the Doctor, 'I threw the stone. My pockets are full of them, look!'

He pulled a handful out of his pocket and showed them.

'Maybe 'e's crazy,' said a woman near me. ' 'E's got an awful queer look in his eye. Come back there, Willie! You keep away from 'im! 'E might bite yer, or something!'

But the constable seemed more puzzled than ever.

'Did you throw it − er − *on purpose*, sir?' he asked in a disbelieving voice.

'Oh, yes, indeed!' said the Doctor brightly. 'Let me show you.'

He took another stone from his pocket and drew back his arm.

'No, no,' said the policeman, hurriedly stopping him. 'You needn't break any more. You can explain to the magistrate. You must come with me. And it's my duty to warn you that anything you say now may be used in evidence against you.'

'Well, just tell me what to say and I'll say it,' said the Doctor eagerly as he moved away at the policeman's side.

'Yes, 'e's crazy all right,' murmured the woman near me. 'Come along, Willie. Time to go home.'

'Maybe he was annoyed because he didn't get asked to the party, Ma,' said Willie.

The commotion inside the house was now

greater than that outside. Maids and footmen
were flying around, pulling down blinds. The
front door was shut and bolted. It looked as
though they feared a bombardment of stones from
the crowd.

As soon as the Doctor and the policeman had got
to the outskirts of the mob I began following
them, keeping a hundred yards or so behind. This
was not difficult because the helmet of the tall
constable could be easily seen at quite a distance.
It was clearly the policeman's intention to avoid
people following, because he took back streets
instead of main ones.

After a little I decided it was no longer
necessary for me to keep back out of the way. The
deed was done now and the Doctor need no longer
fear that I would be accused of having a hand in
it. So presently, when the pair were going
through a quiet little alley, I overtook them.

The constable asked me who I was and what I
wanted. I explained that I was a friend of the man
he had arrested and I wished to go with them to
the police-station. To this he made no objection
and the three of us marched on together.

'Stubbins,' said the Doctor, 'can't *you* think of
something I could say which will be used in
evidence against me?'

'I don't imagine there will be any need for that,'
I said.

The constable just raised his eyebrows, looking
more mystified than ever. He probably thought he
ought to be taking us before a doctor instead of
a magistrate.

Presently we arrived at the Court House and

were taken inside. At a tall desk, like a pulpit, an elderly man was writing in a book. He looked very dignified and severe.

'What's the charge?' he said without looking up.

'Breaking windows, Your Honour,' said the constable.

The magistrate put down his pen and gazed at the three of us through shaggy grey eyebrows.

'Who, the boy?' he asked, jerking his head towards me.

'No, Your Honour,' said the constable. 'The old gentleman here.'

The magistrate put on his glasses and peered scowling, at John Dolittle.

'Do you plead guilty or not guilty?' he asked.

'Guilty, Your Honour,' said the Doctor firmly.

'I don't understand,' murmured the magistrate. 'You – at *your* time of life! Breaking windows! What did you do it for?'

The Doctor was suddenly overcome with embarrassment. He blushed again; shuffled his feet; coughed.

Come, come!' said the magistrate. 'You must have had some reason. Do you hold any grudge against the owner of the house?'

'Oh, no,' said the Doctor. 'None whatever. I didn't even know whose place it was.'

'Are you a glazier? Do you repair windows? – I mean, were you looking for a job?'

'Oh, no,' said the Doctor, more uncomfortable than ever.

'Then why did you do it?'

'I – er – did it – er – just for a lark, Your Honour!' said the Doctor, smiling blandly.

His Honour sat up as though someone had stuck a pin in him.

'For a *lark*!' he thundered. 'And do you think the people of this town consider it a lark to have their houses damaged in this ruffianly manner? A lark! Well, if you are trying to be funny at the expense of the Law we will have to teach you a lesson. What is your calling – I mean what do you do – when you're not breaking windows?'

At this question poor John Dolittle looked as though he was about to sink into the floor.

'I am a doctor,' he said in a very low voice.

'A doctor! Ah!' cried the magistrate. 'Perhaps you hoped to get some patients – bombarding a house with stones! You ought to be ashamed of yourself. Well, you have admitted the charge. So far as I know it's a first offence. But I shall inflict the severest penalty that the law allows me. You are fined five pounds and costs!'

'But I haven't any money,' said the Doctor, brightening up.

'Humph!' snorted His Honour. 'Can't you borrow funds? Have you no friends?'

'No friends with money,' said the Doctor, glancing at me with a hopeful smile.

'I see,' said the magistrate, taking up his pen. 'In that case the law gives me no choice. The court regrets the necessity of imposing this sentence on a man of your years and profession. But you have brought it on yourself and you certainly deserve a lesson. In default of the fine you must go to jail for thirty days.'

The Doctor gave a big sigh of relief. He shook me warmly by the hand. 'Splendid! We've done it,

Stubbins!' he whispered as he picked up his satchel.

There was a knocking on the door. Another policeman entered. Behind him was a large flouncy sort of woman wearing many pearls. With her was a coachman, also a footman. The magistrate got up at once and came down out of his pulpit to greet her.

'Ah, Lady Matilda Beamish!' he cried. 'Come in. What can we do for you?'

'Oh, good heavens!' I heard the Doctor groan behind me.

'I do hope, Your Honour,' said the lady, 'that I'm not too late. I came as fast as I could. It was in my house that the window was broken. Is the trial over? I thought you would need me as a witness.'

'The case has been already dealt with,' said the magistrate. 'The accused pleaded guilty – so there was no need of witnesses beyond the constable who made the arrest.'

'Oh, I was so upset!' said the woman, fluttering a lace handkerchief before her face. 'We were holding the monthly meeting of the County Chapter of the Society for the Prevention of Cruelty to Animals. Refreshments had been served and we were just about to call the meeting to business when a large stone came flying through the drawing-room window and dropped right into the punch bowl. Oh, it was terrible! Sir Willoughby Wiffle was splashed all over! As for myself, I positively swooned away.'

She sank down into a seat and the coachman and footman stood about her, fanning her. The magistrate sent one of the policemen to get a glass of water.

'Dear Lady Matilda,' he said, 'I cannot tell you how sorry I am this outrage should have occurred at your home. However, the prisoner has defaulted on his fine and he is being sent to jail. It will teach him a lesson. I just have to book some particulars. I will be with you in a moment.'

Up to this the woman had been so busy, gasping and fluttering and talking, she had not even looked at the Doctor or myself. Now, when the magistrate left her to go back to his pulpit, she saw us for the first time. The Doctor turned quickly away from her gaze. But she sprang up and cried out, 'Your Honour, is *that* the man who broke my window?'

'Yes,' said the magistrate, 'that is he. Why? Do you know him?'

'*Know* him!' cried Lady Matilda Beamish, bursting into smiles and gurgles of joy. 'Why, I *dote* on him! My *dear* Doctor Dolittle, I am delighted to see you again! But tell me, why didn't you come into the meeting, instead of throwing a stone in instead?'

'I didn't know it was your house,' said the Doctor sheepishly.

The woman turned gushingly to the magistrate.

'Oh, Your Honour,' she cried, 'this is the most wonderful man in the world. A doctor – that is, he was a doctor, but he turned to animals instead. Well, five years ago Topsy, my prize French poodle, had puppies. And she was dreadfully ill – so were the puppies, all of them. The sweetest little things you ever saw – but, oh, so ill! I sent for all the vets in the country. It was no use. Topsy and her children got worse and worse. I wept over them for nights on end. Then I heard about Doctor Dolittle and sent for him. He cured them completely, the whole family. All the puppies won prizes in the show. Oh, I'm so happy to see you again, Doctor! Tell me, where are you living now?'

'In jail,' said John Dolittle, 'or, that is, I expect to be, for a while.'

'In jail!' cried the lady. 'Oh, the window – of course. I had forgotten about that. But let me see,' – she had turned to the magistrate again – 'wasn't there something said about a fine?'

'Yes,' said His Honour. 'Five pounds. The prisoner was unable to pay it. He was sentenced to thirty days in jail instead.'

'Oh, good gracious!' cried the lady. 'We can't have that. I'll pay the fine for him. Atkins, go and bring me my purse. I left it in the carriage.

The footman bowed and went out.

The Doctor came forward quickly.

'It's awfully good of you, Lady Matilda,' he began, 'but I–'

'Now, Doctor, Doctor,' said she, shaking a fat finger at him, 'don't thank me. We can't possibly let you go to jail. It will be a pleasure for me to pay it. In fact, I'm not sure I wouldn't have considered it a privilege to have my window broken, if I had only known it was you who had done it. A very great man,' she whispered aside to the magistrate, 'a little odd and – er – eccentric, but a very great man. I'm so glad I got here in time.'

The purse was brought by the footman and the

money was counted out. The Doctor made several more attempts to interfere but he stood no chance of getting himself heard against the voice of the grateful, talkative lady who was determined to rescue him from jail.

'Very well,' said the magistrate finally, 'the fine is paid and the prisoner is released from custody – with a caution. This was a particularly flagrant breach of the law and it is to be hoped that the prisoner will take the lesson to heart. The Court wishes to express the opinion that the lady against whose premises and property the offence was committed has acted in more than a generous manner in paying the fine imposed.'

The policeman beckoned to the Doctor and me. He led us down a passage, opened a door, and showed us out – into the street.

# Chapter Eleven
## IN JAIL AT LAST

IT was almost twilight now and both the Doctor and I were hungry. Feeling that nothing more could be done that day we set off to tramp the seven miles back to Puddleby and supper. For quite a while neither of us spoke.

At last, when we were nearly home, the Doctor said, 'You know, Stubbins, I almost wish I had followed Matthew's advice and – er – pushed a policeman in the face. It would have been so much – er – so much safer. Did you hear what that woman said – almost a privilege to have her window broken by me? Good heavens! And you know, it was the simplest case, her Topsy and the pups. All I did was give them some digestive pills – an invention of my own – and get their precious mistress to stop fussing over them and leave them in peace. Topsy told me that Lady Matilda was just driving them all crazy, buzzing round them like a bee and giving them the stupidest things to eat. I forbade her go near the dogs for a week and they got all right – on milk. Ah, well!'

There was great excitement when we reached
the house and stepped in at the kitchen door.

'Why, Doctor!' squeaked the white mouse,
'didn't you go to jail, then?'

'No,' said the Doctor, sinking miserably into a
chair, 'but Matthew did. I feel perfectly terrible
about it. I must go over and see his wife Theodosia
in the morning. I don't suppose she'll ever be able
to forgive me.'

'Matthew! In jail!' said Too-Too. 'Why, I saw
him out in the scullery just now, washing his
hands.'

'You must be mistaken,' said the Doctor. 'The
last we saw of him was in Gilesborough. He was
being marched off to prison. He threw a stone into
the window of the bank, hoping that the people
would think it was me. But they didn't. He was
arrested.'

At that moment the door into the pantry opened
and Matthew entered smiling.

' 'Ullo, Doctor,' said he cheerily. 'So they
wouldn't take you in up at Gilesborough jail, eh?
Too bad! Most in'ospitable of 'em, I calls it – most
in'ospitable!'

'But, look here, Matthew,' said the Doctor, 'what
about yourself? Do you mean to say they turned
you away too?'

'Hoh, no!' grinned the cats'-meat-man. 'They
never turns me away – not from jails. But you
see, on the way to the police-station I 'appened to
remember that I 'adn't got me skeleton key with
me. And though I could, most likely, 'ave got
myself out of that jail without hartificial means,
I thought maybe it would be best to be on the safe

side and escape *before* I got to jail. So I sizes up the copper what was takin' me along, see? And I notices 'e was a kind of 'eavy-built bloke, no good for runnin' at all. So with great foresight and hindsight – still goin' along peaceful with 'im like – I picks out a spot to shake 'im. You know that fountain on the green with the big marble pool around it?'

'Yes,' said the Doctor, 'I remember it.'

'Well, just as we comes alongside o' that pool I says to 'im, I says, "Why, sergeant!" – I knew 'e was only a constable, but they all likes to be called sergeant – "Why, sergeant," I says, "look, yer bootlace is untied." 'E bends down to look – and, bein' very fat, 'e 'ad to bend away down to see 'is feet. Then I gives 'im a gentle shove from the rear and in 'e goes, 'ead-first, into the marble pool. Ha! Just as neat as a divin' walrus. Then I dashes off across the green and down an alley. I took to the open country as soon as I got a chance. And, well – 'ere I am!'

'Humph!' said the Doctor. 'Good gracious me! Anyway, I'm glad you're safe and sound, Matthew. I was very worried about you. What have we got for supper, Dab-Dab?'

'Fried eggs, cheese, tomatoes and cocoa,' said the housekeeper.

'A-a-a-h!' said Gub-Gub, coming up to the table. 'Tomatoes!'

'Um-m-m-m, cocoa!' said Chee-Chee. 'Good idea!'

'And cheese, hooray!' squeaked the white mouse, scrambling down from the mantelpiece.

'You know, Matthew,' said the Doctor when we were seated at the meal, 'I think we had better leave Gilesborough alone. What with you giving a policeman in uniform a bath, and my fine being paid by the most prominent lady in the town, I feel we'd better stay away from there. In fact, I'm very discouraged about the whole business. As I told Stubbins, I had no idea it was so hard to get into jail.'

'Well, yer see, Doctor,' said Matthew, buttering large slabs of bread, 'that's the way it is: when yer wants to get into jail they won't 'ave yer, and when you don't want to get into jail, they takes yer and puts yer there. The whole law, I might say, is a very himperfect hinstrument. But don't you be down-'earted, Doctor. Keep up the good work! After all, yer did get arrested this last shot, and yer didn't even get that far the first time. You see, you got the beginnings of a reputation now. It's easy to get into jail when you got the right reputation.'

Polynesia, sitting on the window-sill, let out a short 'Huh!'

'Yes, but just the same,' said the Doctor, 'I don't think we should use Gilesborough any more for our – er – experiments.'

'That's all right, Doctor,' said Matthew, reaching for the cheese. 'There's lots of other places. Your reputation will spread. Wonderful 'ow a good jail reputation gets around. Now listen: there's Goresby-St. Clements, pretty little town – and a good jail, too! And I was thinkin' – should 'ave thought of it before – the best thing for you to do is not to bother with banks and charity meetin's this time. Just go and bust the window of the police-station itself – or the Court 'Ouse,

' "The whole law, I might say, is a very himperfect
hinstrument" '

whichever yer fancy. They'll be bound to lock you up then!'

'Humph!' said the Doctor. 'Er – yes, that sounds a good idea.'

'I'll come along with yer, Doctor,' said Matthew. 'You might not be able to–'

'No, Matthew,' said the Doctor firmly. 'I am afraid you may get arrested again by mistake. In fact, I don't believe I'll even take Stubbins with me this time. I'll go alone. It will be safer.'

'All right, Doctor,' said Matthew, 'anyway, what makes you most comfortable. But you will see there ain't no bunglin', won't yer? And don't forget, choose the police-station, or the Court 'Ouse, when the judge is there. Use a good big stone, too. My, but I'd love to see it! When will we be hearin' from yer?'

'You *won't* be hearing from me – if I get into jail,' said the Doctor. 'But you will if I don't.'

The next morning John Dolittle set out for Goresby-St Clements. This was another long walk from Puddleby and for that reason he made an early start. Dab-Dab had provided him with a large packet of sandwiches and a bottle of milk. He also took with him a good supply of writing-paper and lots of pencils – and of course his notes.

I went down the road a little way with him to see him off. He seemed very happy and hopeful as he bade me goodbye. The last thing he said was, 'Stubbins, if I'm not back here by midnight you'll know I've succeeded. Don't bother about visiting me for a good while. And on no account let Matthew come at all. I'll be all right. Look after the old lame horse. And keep an eye on those moon plants for me. So long!'

Well, that time he did succeed – as we heard later. All the animals insisted on sitting up with me that night to see if John Dolittle would return. When the old clock in the hall struck midnight we knew that he was in jail at last. Then I sent them off to bed.

# Chapter Twelve
## ITTY

**F**OR the next few days I was kept very busy. Without the Doctor in the house I felt entirely responsible that everything should go well. And there was much more to attend to now than when I had been in charge before.

For one thing, there were the animal patients. Although the number of these calling at the house daily fell off, as soon as it was known that the Doctor was away from home, the sick animals did not by any means stop coming. They all wanted to know where the Doctor had gone. I refused to tell them. Then some of them asked me to give them more of this medicine, or that ointment, which they had been getting before from the Doctor. Next thing, a few who had cuts and bruises asked if I would treat their troubles, since the Doctor was no longer there. Of course in my years of helping John Dolittle in this sort of work I had learned a lot. I bandaged them up and even set a broken bone or two.

I got very interested in the work. I felt proud that I could handle sick cases all by myself. Then I began to notice that the line waiting outside the dispensary door wasn't getting any less each morning, as it had at the start. Once in a while a more difficult case would come in, needing pretty ticklish surgery. I wished the Doctor was there to help me. But he wasn't. Some of these were urgent cases that needed attention at once. There was no one else to handle the work, so I did it.

I began to study John Dolittle's books, volumes he had written on animal medicine and animal surgery. I took on more and more difficult tricks of doctoring – sometimes with my heart in my mouth, scared to death the poor creatures might die under my hands. But none of them did – thank goodness!

Without doubt I was very lucky in this. But also it must not be forgotten that I was greatly helped by knowing animal languages – I was the only one (at that time) besides the great man himself who did. I noticed that more and more the animal patients seemed to have confidence in me. Even when I had to put a stitch in a bad cut they lay wonderfully still, apparently knowing that I would save them all the pain I possibly could.

I began to ask myself where all this might lead me to. My reputation among the animals was growing – the same as the Doctor's had done when he first left the profession of human medicine and took to the care of the animal world. I don't mean to say that I dreamed for one moment that I could take the great man's place. No one living could ever have done that. But as I got busier and busier with the work of the dispensary I did begin to wonder – if the Doctor

should stay long enough in prison — whether I too
might some day have to run away and hide to get
peace and quiet. Anyhow it can be easily
understood how a young boy would be tremen-
dously thrilled to find he was doing even as much
as I was to carry on the work of so important a
person.

But besides my duties as assistant doctor there
were plenty of other things to keep me on the go.
There were the animal clubs down in the zoo. I
had to keep an eye on Jip and Flip so that they
didn't bring in too many new members for the
'Home'. Feeding them properly these days was the
big problem. It required money to do that. (My job
as book-keeper for the butcher had to be kept
going too, or there wouldn't have been any money
at all.)

And then that blessed little Whitey! In spite of
his small size he was all over the place at the
same time, poking his cheeky pink nose into
everything. He seemed to discover a new family
of wild mice or rats every day. He would come to
me with a long sad story of their troubles and ask
if they could join the Rat and Mouse Club —
which I usually found they had done already,
before I had given permission.

And I had to take care of the moon plants. This
was a big job — keeping notes on weather conditions, rate of growth and goodness knows what
more. But this was one of the departments of our
establishment which could not be neglected on
any account. Not only had the Doctor on leaving
instructed me to give it special attention, but I
knew that the raising of these food-stuffs from the

Moon would be necessary for his experiments later on and for the writing of his book. He felt that the very secret of everlasting life itself might be contained in these seeds of vegetables and fruits which he had brought down from that other world. If I let the plants die while he was away, he would never be able to try them out on the creatures of the Earth.

And then there was Itty, the moon cat — strangest and most puzzling of animals. True, she did not demand any of my time, but I became very interested in her. She had not yet taken her place as part of the household (for which the rest of the animals were not sorry). But she was now at least willing to leave her cage. And she used to wander round the garden on silent feet, examining everything with great care and curiosity. She seemed particularly interested in the birds and watched them by the hour. This frightened the birds a good deal, especially those who were late nesters and still had young ones to raise. But Itty seemed to remember her promise to the Doctor, for I never saw her kill or even try to catch one.

Occasionally at night I would see her looking up at the Moon, wistfully — as though she was wondering what was going on there, in that home world of hers from which she had cut herself off with so much courage. The other animals, when she first came out and began to move about, left her severely alone. They sneaked into corners when they saw her coming, and kept out of her way. Her answer to this was to keep out of *their* way — but in a superior, far grander manner. It seemed almost as though, having lived so many thousands of years longer than these upstart earth animals, she felt she should meet their rude unfriendliness with dignity instead of anger — rather the way one might leave impertinent, naughty children to grow older and learn better manners.

Certainly I have never known an animal who had such complete confidence in herself. She always seemed to be mistress of the situation, whatever happened. Her eyes! This world of ours has never seen anything like them. In the dark they didn't just glow, they burned and smouldered with a light of their own. When they looked into your own eyes, steadily, for minutes on end, they seemed to be reading your thoughts, searching you and your whole life — all the lives that lay behind you, your father's, your grandfather's, back to the beginning of time. Itty, often uncomfortable company perhaps, was for me always fascinating.

Quite a while before this I had learned something of her language. She talked very little — gave no opinions. She appeared to be feeling her way about this new world, so to speak, before she would say what she thought of it. When I told her that the Doctor had gone away she seemed quite upset. But I assured her at once that he would be back before very long.

From them on she tried in her funny stiff way to show me that she liked me. This I am sure was not just because I fed her, but because I always treated her in the way she liked to be treated. Of her own accord she would often follow me round the place and watch with great interest whatever

I was doing. But she had never as yet gone into the house.

One evening when I was returning from some of my gardening work I found her sitting on the Long Lawn gazing at the Moon. I asked her if she would not like to come inside and join the animals round the kitchen fire. Rather to my surprise, she came in with me right away without saying a word.

In the kitchen they were all there: Gub-Gub, Chee-Chee, Dab-Dab, Polynesia, Jip, Too-Too and Whitey. They greeted me with friendly shouts, but when poor Itty stalked in behind me they all bristled like a lot of porcupines and a dead silence fell over the room.

The cat went over everything in the kitchen with her usual careful inspection. On the bottom shelf of the dresser there was a sort of rack for pots and pans. She peered into all the pots and smelt each of the pans. She moved silently over to the fireplace and examined the poker and tongs as though wondering what they were for. The fire itself she stared at for a long while and I wondered if it was the first time she had seen one burning inside a house.

During all this the rest of the animals never uttered a sound or a word, but followed her round the room with seven pairs of suspicious eyes as though she were a bomb that might blow up, or a creeping, deadly snake. I felt so angry I could have slapped them.

I nudged Jip with my knee and whispered.

'Can't you say something, you duffer? Start a

little conversation. I never saw such hospitality. Make her feel at home!'

Jip coughed and spluttered and grunted like some one coming out of a trance.

'Oh, ah, yes,' he said. 'Er – ahem – er – splendid weather we're having, eh?'

I made signs to the rest of them to wake up and show some life. Gub-Gub came to the conversational rescue.

'Yes, indeed,' said he, 'though I did think it might rain in the early part of the morning. But who cares? There will be lots more weather tomorrow.'

I glanced for help towards Polynesia on the window-sill. She looked as sour as a pickle, but she understood I wanted entertainment. She broke into a dismal Russian sea-song about a shipwreck.

Then Whitey started to tell jokes, particularly dull ones which no one apparently heard – and even he himself forgot to laugh at them. Everybody's eyes and attention were still on the cat, who continued to stalk round the room. She looked as though she were taking no notice whatever of anything but her tour of inspection. Yet I felt certain she was listening to every word that was being said, and, quite possibly, understanding a good deal of it.

Finally she disappeared under the table. Then all the company became more uncomfortable and awkward than ever. When they couldn't see her they seemed to feel their very lives were in danger from a hidden enemy. I truly believe that if I had not been there they would have broken

and run off in a panic. I was furious with them,
knowing how much John Dolittle wanted the
moon cat to feel at home in his house. Things
were going from bad to worse. I did some chattering myself, talking about anything that came into
my head. It was hard, uphill work. But I did
manage to bully them at least into making a
noise. It was the most ridiculous kind of conversation, but it was better than nothing.

After several minutes of it Dab-Dab said,

'Sh! What's that noise?'

We all listened. It *was* a strange sound.

'It's almost like a strong wind in the trees,'
whispered Gub-Gub.

'More like the sea breaking on a beach,' said Jip.

'No – an engine, I'd say,' murmured Dab-Dab.
'Or a band playing in the distance –
Extraordinary!'

'I wonder where it's coming from,' squeaked the
white mouse, who had, as usual, retired to the
mantelpiece.

I looked under the table.

It was Itty. Although her eyes were half closed,
I thought I saw the shadow of a smile on her face.

*She was purring!*

# Chapter Thirteen
## IN THE DOCTOR'S CELL

BUT in spite of all there was to do, the old place was not the same without John Dolittle. I missed him terribly – so did the animals. The chats around the kitchen fire after supper were not the same. Somebody would start a story and we would all begin by listening attentively. Yet sooner or later the interest would wear off, the thoughts of the listeners would stray and we would end by talking about the Doctor and wondering how he was getting on.

Dab-Dab, Too-Too, Jip and Chee-Chee – although they missed him as keenly as any – did not seem to worry about him so much. They were old and experienced friends of John Dolittle. They felt that he could take care of himself and would send us news of how he was getting on as soon as it was convenient for him to do so. But Gub-Gub and the white mouse began to get very upset as day after day went by and no news came from Goresby-St Clements. They took me aside one morning when I was attending to the moon plants. (Polynesia was with me at the time.) They both looked very serious.

'Tell me, Tommy,' said Gub-Gub, 'when are you planning to visit the Doctor?'

'Oh,' said I, 'I hadn't set any exact date. But he especially asked me to leave him alone for a good while. He's afraid that the police may find out that he got in jail on purpose. He wants to get sort of settled down before he has any visitors.'

'Settled down!' cried the white mouse. 'That sounds as though he might be there a terribly long time.'

'We don't even know,' said Gub-Gub with a very worried look, 'how long they sent him to prison for. Maybe they sent him to jail for life!'

'Oh, no, Gub-Gub,' I said, laughing. 'They don't send people to prison for life – except for terribly serious crimes.'

'But we haven't *heard*,' squeaked the white mouse. 'Maybe he did do something serious. He wasn't very successful with the window-breaking business. Perhaps he got desperate and killed a policeman – or a judge – just by accident I mean. Who knows?'

'No, no,' I said, 'that's not at all likely. If he got a sentence of a month in jail, that would be the most. And he would consider himself lucky to get that.'

'But we don't *know*, Tommy, do we?' said the white mouse. 'This – er – uncertainty is very wearing. We've heard nothing since he left. I can hardly sleep worrying about it, and ordinarily I'm a very good sleeper – at least I was until you brought that terrible cat into the house. But I do wish we had some word of how he is.'

'What is he getting to eat?' asked Gub-Gub.

'They took me aside one morning'

'I've no idea,' I said, 'but enough, anyhow, I'm sure.'

'When we were thrown into jail by the King of the Jolliginki in Africa,' said Gub-Gub, 'we weren't given anything to eat at all!'

'Fiddlesticks!' snorted Polynesia, who was sitting on a tree near by. 'We got put in prison after lunch and we escaped again before supper-time. What do you expect in jail – *four* meals a day?'

'Well, we didn't get anything to eat while we were in prison,' said Whitey. 'Gub-Gub's right. I was there too and I know. Something should be done about the Doctor. I'm worried.'

'Oh, mind your own business!' said Polynesia. 'The Doctor will take care of himself. You're a fuss-budget.'

As a matter of fact I was beginning to be a little bit disturbed about the Doctor myself. Although he had told me he would 'be all right' I was anxious to hear how he was getting on. But that same afternoon Cheapside, the London sparrow, came to pay a visit. He was of course very interested to hear what had happened to his friend. When I told him that the Doctor had gone to jail to write a book he chuckled with delight.

'Well, if that ain't like 'im!' said he. 'Jail!'

'Listen, Cheapside,' said I, 'if you're not busy perhaps you'd fly over to Goresby and see what you can find out.'

'You bet,' said Cheapside. 'I'll go over right away.'

The sparrow disappeared without another word. He was back again about tea-time – as was

usual with him. And I was mighty glad to see
him. I took him into the study where we could
talk privately. He had seen the Doctor, he told me
– got through the bars of his prison window and
had a long chat with him.

'How did he look, Cheapside?' I asked eagerly.

'Oh, pretty good,' said the sparrow. 'You know
John Dolittle – 'e always keeps up, But 'e said 'e'd
like ter see yer, Tommy. 'E wants some more of
his notes. And 'e's used up all the pencils 'e took
with 'im. "Tell Stubbins," 'e said, "there ain't no
special 'urry but I would like to see 'im. Ask 'im
to come over about the end of the week – say
Sunday." '

'How is he otherwise?' I asked. 'Is he getting
enough to eat and all that?'

'Well,' said Cheapside, 'I can't say as 'ow 'is
board and lodgin' is any too elegant. 'E 'ad a kind
of thing to sleep on – sort of a cot, you'd call it,
I suppose. But it looked to me more like an ironin'
board. Grub? Well, there again, o' course 'e didn't
complain. 'E wouldn't. You know John Dolittle –
the really important things o' life never did seem
to hinterest 'im. 'E'd eat what was given 'im and
ask no questions. You know 'ow 'e is!'

At this moment I heard a scuttling among the
book-shelves.

'What was that noise, Cheapside?' I asked.

'Sounded to me like a mouse,' said he.

Starting out early on Sunday morning I reached
Goresby jail about eleven o'clock. I noticed as I
entered the building that many labourers were
digging at the side of one wall, as if they were at
work on the foundations.

Inside, a policeman booked my name at the desk and made out a pass for me as a visitor. As he gave it to me he said, 'Young man, I think you're maybe just in time.'

'Pardon me,' I said, 'just in time? I don't quite understand.'

'The superintendent,' he said. 'He's awful mad. He wants to have the prisoner Dolittle removed.'

I was about to ask him why the superintendent wished to get rid of the Doctor. But at that moment another policeman led me away to my friend's cell.

It was a strange room. The high walls were made of stone. There was a window near the ceiling. Seated on the bed which was littered with papers John Dolittle was writing fast and furiously. He was so taken up with his work that he did not seem to notice our coming in. The policeman went out again right away and, locking the door behind him, left us together.

Still the Doctor did not look up. It was only when I started to make my way across to where he sat that I noticed the condition of the floor. It was paved with cobblestones – or rather, I should say, it had been. Now it looked like a street which had been taken up by workmen. The whole floor was broken into big holes and all the cobblestones lay around higgledy-piggledy. Littered among these were scraps of food, pieces of cheese, hunks of bread, radishes – even chop-bones, looking the worse for wear.

'Why, Doctor,' I asked, touching him gently on the shoulder, 'what's happened here?'

'Oh, hullo, Stubbins,' said he. 'Well, I hardly

know – er – that is, not exactly. You see I've
been so busy. But it seems that I'm going to have
to leave very soon.'

'Why, Doctor?' I asked. 'Why? What has
happened?'

'Well,' said he, 'everything went fine until three
days ago. I had done my best. I broke all the windows in the front of the police-station. I was
arrested at once. They gave me a sentence of
thirty days in jail, and I thought everything was
all right. I set to work on the book and I got a good
deal done. Everything was going splendidly. And
then, Wednesday – I believe it was Wednesday –
a mouse came in and visited me. Yes, I know
you'd think it was impossible, with all these stone
walls. But he got in somehow. Then more came,
rats too. They seemed to burrow under the
corners, everywhere. They brought me food. They
said they had come to set me free.'

'But how did they know you were here?' I cried.
'It has been kept a dead secret.'

'I've no idea,' he said. 'I asked them, but they
wouldn't tell me. Then after the mice had fetched
up a lot of rats, the rats went off and fetched a
whole lot of badgers. They brought me food, too
– all sorts of stuff. Apparently they did not think
I was getting enough to eat. The badgers began
digging a tunnel under the prison wall to let me
out by. I begged them to leave the place alone, but
they wouldn't listen. Their minds were made up
that it wasn't good for me to stay in jail. And
there you are. . . . Sit down, Stubbins, sit down!'

I moved some of the papers aside on the bed and
made room for myself.

'When the police discovered what a mess had been made,' he went on, 'they moved me into another cell, this one here. But the same thing happened again. The rats and badgers came tunnelling in at night under the walls.'

'But, Doctor,' said I, 'outside, as I came in, they told me something about the superintendent. What does it mean?'

'It means, I fear,' he said, 'that I'm going to get put out of the prison altogether. After all my work in getting in here! And my book isn't one-quarter done yet!'

As the Doctor finished speaking we heard the rattling of a key in the lock. Two policemen entered. One I could see from his uniform was a superior officer of some kind. He held a paper in his hand.

'John Dolittle,' he said, 'I have here an order for your release.'

'But, Superintendent,' said the Doctor, 'I was sentenced to thirty days. I've hardly been here half that time.'

'I can't help it,' said the superintendent. 'The whole building is falling down. A new crack has just shown up in the guardroom wall – all the way from floor to ceiling. We've called the architect in and he says the whole jail is going to be wrecked if something isn't done. So we've got a special order from the court withdrawing the charge against you.'

'But look here,' said the Doctor, 'you must admit I was a very well-behaved prisoner. All this disturbance was not my fault.'

'I don't know anything about that,' said the

superintendent. 'Whether these were your own trained circus animals that did the mischief is not the point. I've been in charge here for seven years now and nothing like this ever happened before. We've got to save the jail. The charge is withdrawn and out you've got to go.'

'Dear, dear!' sighed the Doctor, 'and just when I was getting so comfortably settled and everything. I don't know what I'll do now, really I don't.'

He looked again at the superintendent as if he hoped he might relent and change his mind. But all that gentleman said was, 'Get your things packed up now. We've got to let the workmen in here to relay this floor.'

Miserably the Doctor put his papers together and I helped him pack them into the satchel. When we were ready the police once again showed us, very politely, to the door and freedom.

# Chapter Fourteen
## THE LITTLE VILLAIN

WE got back home about three in the afternoon.

Once again the whole household wanted to know what had happened – all of them, that is, except Whitey. I noticed that he was not among the welcoming committee who met us in the garden.

When the Doctor was inside the house he explained why he had come back so soon.

'Did you say your first visitor was a mouse, Doctor?' asked Dab-Dab suspiciously.

'Yes,' said the Doctor. 'First one and then hundreds – then rats and then badgers. They turned the whole jail upside down. It will cost the police hundreds of pounds to put the building right again. I really can't blame them for wanting to get rid of me. But just the same it was very provoking, most annoying – just when I was getting into a nice swing with my book and everything was going splendidly. You see, I had planned, after they would turn me loose at the end of my thirty days, to break another window and come in again for a new sentence. But there wouldn't have been much use in trying to do any more harm to *that* police-station. The mice and rats and badgers had positively wrecked the place already.'

'Humph! Mice, eh?' said Polynesia. 'I smell a mouse myself now – a white mouse. Where's Whitey?'

I suddenly remembered the noise I had heard behind the books when I had been talking to Cheapside.

'Yes,' I said, 'where *is* Whitey?'

A general search for that inquisitive little animal was made at once. Too-Too discovered him hiding behind an egg-cup in the china cupboard. He was brought out looking very ashamed of himself and quite scared. Dab-Dab seemed to be the one he was most afraid of. He immediately scrambled up on to the mantelpiece to get out of her reach. Dab-Dab positively bristled with anger as she came forward to talk to him.

'Now,' she said, 'tell us: did you have anything to do with this?'

'With what?' asked the white mouse, trying very hard to look innocent but making a poor job of it.

'With all these mice and rats and badgers going to the prison to set the Doctor free?' snapped the duck. 'Come on now – out with it. What do you know?'

The housekeeper stretched up her neck towards the small culprit with such blazing anger in her eyes that for a moment it looked as though she was going to gobble him up. Poor Whitey was absolutely terrified.

'Well,' he gasped, 'you see, Gub-Gub and I –'

'Oh, so Gub-Gub was in it too, was he?' said Dab-Dab. 'Where's that pig?'

But Gub-Gub had apprently thought it wiser to go off gardening. At any rate he could not be found in the house.

'Go on then, go on,' said Dab-Dab. 'What did you and that precious Gub-Gub do?'

'We didn't really do anything,' said Whitey. 'But – er – well, you see – er – we couldn't find out how the Doctor was getting on over there at Goresby-St Clements. No one could tell us even whether he was getting enough to eat or not. We knew that the food in prisons isn't usually very good. So we – er – well, I–'

'Yes, go on!' Dab-Dab hissed.

'I thought it would be a good idea to talk it over with the members of the Rat and Mouse Club,' said Whitey.

Dab-Dab looked as though she was going to have a fit.

'So!' she snorted. 'You knew perfectly well it was to be kept a secret – where the Doctor had gone and everything – and yet you went down and gabbled your silly little head off at the Rat and Mouse Club!'

'But don't you see,' wailed Whitey, real tears coming into his pink eyes, 'don't you see we didn't know what had happened to him? For all we knew he might have been put in jail for life. When we had talked it over at the club the old Prison Rat – you remember, the one who told us that story years ago – he said, "John Dolittle should be set free right away." He didn't tell us then how he was going to do it. But he is a very old and cunning rat – frightfully experienced where prisons are concerned. And we trusted him.'

'Oh,' said Dab-Dab. 'Well, will you be good enough to tell us what happened next?'

Then Whitey explained how the old Prison Rat (who in his day had set free an innocent man from jail by carrying a file in to him, so that he could cut his window-bars) had taken charge of the situation and acted as commander-in-chief in this plot to set the Doctor free.

Rats and mice are curious folk. They live in the houses and homes of people although they are not wanted there – and they know it. But they listen behind the panelling or under the floors, and they hear everything and know what is going on. They know everything, because they are always listening.

And so the Prison Rat, that old grey-haired veteran of many adventures, had engineered the whole thing. Directly Whitey had spoken at the club about his fears, this general had laid his plans without asking further questions. All the underground machinery of the world of rats and mice was set in motion. Word was sent out that the beloved John Dolittle, the man who had cured the sicknesses of all the animal world, was locked up in a town called Goresby-St Clements.

The troops were mustered immediately – at first only mice and rats. The message was sent from house to house. Then the field mice were called on and the news flew across country from town to town. John Dolittle was in danger! The message reached Goresby. Larger burrowing animals, like badgers, were needed to pry up the stones of the prison floor. Food was needed! All right. Every larder for miles around was robbed

' "Duffer! Didn't we tell you it was to be kept a secret?" '

of slices of cheese, pieces of bread, apples, bananas – anything. The great man must have food. At night, when only a few policemen were on guard, the army set to work and drilled tunnels under the prison walls. And that was how Goresby jail had been wrecked.

When Whitey finished his story there was a short silence. Suddenly I heard something outside. I could see from the Doctor's face that he heard it too. It came from the bottom of the garden. It was a most peculiar noise. To any ordinary ears it was just a lot of squeaks – loud squeaks. But to us who knew animal languages it meant something more. It was coming from the Rat and Mouse Club down in the zoo. A party – a very noisy party – was going on, to celebrate the Doctor's home-coming. We listened. Speeches were being made. There was a lot of applause as one speaker ended and another began. Cheers – and more cheers. Now we could even make out the words in the distance: 'Hooray! Hooray! The Doctor's back home again! Hear, hear! Hooray! . . . Who brought him back? Who set him free? The Prison Rat! . . . Three cheers for the Doctor! Three cheers for the Prison Rat! . . . Hooray, hooray, hooray!'

The voices trailed off and faded away. Dab-Dab turned again to scold Whitey.

'You little villain!' she began, 'I could–'

'Oh, never mind, never mind,' said the Doctor. 'Leave him alone, Dab-Dab. The harm is done now. And anyway it was the Prison Rat who was probably responsible for most of it. Whitey thought he was acting for the best, no doubt. Let bygones be bygones.'

# Chapter Fifteen
## A GRAND PARTY

AT this moment the Doctor was called away to see a patient in the dispensary. I went with him. It was a weasel with a sprained back — not an easy matter to put right at all. I helped the Doctor with the case.

After hours of working on it we got the small creature into a sort of jacket made of twigs, like a tube, so that he couldn't bend his spine in any direction. It looked as though it was very uncomfortable for the weasel. They are naturally squirmy, wriggly things. But this one soon found, when the Doctor had laid him down in one of his little box beds which he kept for cases of this kind, that the pain of his back was greatly eased as long as he did what the Doctor told him to — which was to keep perfectly still. We moved him into the small-animal hospital in the attic.

As we started to go downstairs Chee-Chee met us with the news that a heron was waiting to see him with severe gout trouble in the leg joints.

'There you are, Stubbins,' said John Dolittle, 'you see? What chance is there for me to get this book finished — with all the experiments that have to be made — while I have to look after these patients? I can't neglect them, can I? What am I to do?'

'Look here, Doctor,' said I. 'I have an idea. While you were away many cases came to the house. I told them that you were not here — wouldn't be back for some time. Well, some of them needed attention right away. They asked me to see to them. I was awfully scared at first, afraid I wouldn't do the right thing. But you see, being your assistant so long, I had learned a good deal.'

At this point I noticed Polynesia hopping up the stairs to meet us.

'Some of the cases, Doctor,' I said, 'were quite tricky. But you were not here and I had to take them on. I actually set a wren's broken wing. What do you think of that?'

'Why, Stubbins!' he cried, 'that's splendid! Setting a wing on a bird as small as that is about as delicate a job as I know of. Splendid, splendid! And it came out all right?'

'It certainly did, Doctor,' said Polynesia. 'I was there and I know. Remember, I gave Tommy his first lessons in bird languages, the same as I did to you. I always knew he'd turn out a good naturalist.'

'Now you see, Doctor,' I said, 'there's no reason why you should not turn over the dispensary to me. If any particularly difficult job should come along I can always call you in. But you need not bother with the ordinary work of the patients. Go ahead and write your book in peace here, in your own home. Why not?'

'Er — yes, Stubbins,' he said slowly. 'After all,

why not? An excellent idea! Anyhow, we can see how it works.'

And so the plan was actually tried out. Dab-Dab and Polynesia gave orders to everybody in the household that as soon as a patient appeared at the gate I should be sent for and not the Doctor. I was a little bit scared at first, fearing still that I might make some serious mistakes with the more ticklish cases; and while I was better off than when the Doctor had been away, I did not want to call upon him for help too often.

But on the whole things went very well. I made Chee-Chee and Polynesia my assistants. The monkey was a wonderful help with his small hands. For all such work as rolling narrow bandages (some of them no wider than a shoe-lace) his slender fingers were just the thing. He was, too, a naturally kindly soul and the animal patients liked him. I taught him how to count a pulse with the watch and take temperatures with the thermometer.

Polynesia I used mostly as a special interpreter when difficulties in animal languages cropped up. We often had new and rare animals coming to the dispensary, like bats and voles and bitterns and choughs. And without the old parrot's help it would have been very hard for me to talk with them.

As soon as I had the whole thing running smoothly I must admit I felt very proud – especially when the Doctor came and visited us and said he thought we were doing exceedingly well.

And of course all the members of the household

were more than delighted. They saw now a chance of keeping the beloved Doctor under his own roof for a long time, since he was busy on a book and his experiments in moon vegetables.

One evening just as I was closing up the dispensary they all came to me in a body and asked me to do them a special favour. Naturally I asked them what it was before I made any promises.

'Well, Tommy, it's like this,' said Gub-Gub. 'While we are no end pleased that the Doctor is staying with us for a time, we don't see as much of him as we used to. He sticks at that book all the time. We think he ought to give himself a holiday once in a while. And then again, we miss him awful much at our evening chats over the kitchen fire. You know what splendid stories and disgustings—' ('*Discussions*, you booby, discussions!' snapped Jip in his ear.) 'Yes — er — discussions is what I mean,' Gub-Gub went on. 'And it isn't the same any more now.'

'Yes, I understand that,' I said.

'So we all thought,' said Gub-Gub, 'that it would be a good way to celebrate the Doctor's returning home to ask him to come to one of our after-supper parties in the kitchen — as he used to.'

'And you see, Tommy,' said the white mouse, 'it will be specially nice now because we're well into autumn and we can have a roaring fire.'

'Exactly,' said Gub-Gub. 'Only yesterday I was thinking of covering my spinach' (Gub-Gub always spoke of everything in the garden as 'my' — 'my rhubarb,' 'my parsley,' 'my tomatoes,' etc.). 'We may have frost any day now,' he went on.

after all a fire is a real fire only when there's a
frost in the air. What do you say, Tommy?'

'Well, Gub-Gub,' said I, 'I think it would do the
Doctor good to get away from his work for one
evening. I'll go and talk with him and see what
he says.'

As a matter of fact, it was not easy for me to
persuade the Doctor. I found him in his study,
writing busily as usual. Sheets of papers with
notes on them lay all over the floor; more pieces
of paper were pinned on the walls around his
desk; plates of sandwiches (which the devoted
Dab-Dab brought him three times a day) were scat-
tered round the room, many of them untouched.
I explained to him what the animals had asked
of me.

'Well, Stubbins,' he said. 'I would most willingly
come down to the kitchen after supper – I used
to regularly at one time, you know. But – er –
well – just now it's different. I'm behindhand
with the book. Thought I would have been much
further along with it by this time. And then there
are the experiments with the plants waiting for
me. You see, I'm dividing the book into two parts.
The first part is concerned with my discoveries *on*
the Moon; animal, vegetable and mineral, you
know. I haven't got half-way through that yet. The
second part is about my trying to grow certain
moon things down here on the Earth – mostly
vegetable, but some insect forms. And it is in
that, Stubbins, that I hope to discover some of the
really big secrets – such as the great length of life
up there, almost everlasting life. Yes, perhaps

even that itself – with scientific guidance –
everlasting life!'

'But listen, Doctor,' I said. 'It will do you good
to leave your desk for one evening. The animals
have set their hearts on it. They want to celebrate
your coming back to your own home – to them.
You know, whether you like it or not, they do feel
you belong to them.'

He smiled. Then he laughed. Then he threw his
pencil down on the desk.

'All right, Stubbins,' he said. 'It probably will do
me no harm to get away for a while.'

He rose from his chair and we left the study.

It was indeed a very successful evening.
Everybody was there: Jip, Too-Too, Polynesia,
Chee-Chee, Gub-Gub, Whitey, Dab-Dab and
Cheapside. Matthew Mugg had dropped in again,
so we had him too. And the old lame horse, when
he heard that the Doctor was going to be present,
said he would like to be there. We got him into
the house through the big double doors we had
used for the Doctor when he was still a giant. And
though Dab-Dab was terribly scared that he
would knock the dresser over, we finally managed
to bed him down under the windows where he
could see and hear everything that went on.

And then there was Itty. The moon cat now
came and went about the house without any one's
being afraid of her. I had been amused to notice
that the two who had raised the biggest rumpus
about her at first, Whitey and Jip, had become the
best friends she had in the whole family circle.

Piles and piles of wood had been gathered in the
kitchen and stacked near the hearth. The air was

cold and brisk, and a splendid fire was roaring up
the chimney. Dab-Dab had prepared plates of
sandwiches, hard-boiled eggs, toasted cheese on
biscuits, radishes and glasses of milk. Gub-Gub
had brought for himself a large heap of rosy
autumn apples. (He said he always listened best
on apples.) The big kitchen table looked like a
grand picnic.

When the Doctor came in he was greeted by a
noisy chorus of cheers.

'Ah!' the white mouse whispered to me as he
climbed to his place on the mantelpiece. 'This,
Tommy, is *really* like old times. Hand me up one
of those cheese-biscuits, will you?'

Well, stories were told by everybody, new
stories, old stories, true stories and stories that
might have been true. Jip told one; Too-Too told
one; Chee-Chee told one; the Doctor told four, and
I told two. The white mouse told the latest jokes
from the Rat and Mouse Club. Cheapside gave us
all the up-to-date news from London. Gub-Gub
recited one of his salad poems and another
romantic piece of his own (which we had heard
before) called, 'Meet Me on the Garbage Heap
When the Moon Is Hanging Low.' And old
Polynesia sang us sea-songs in five different
languages. I have never heard so much laughing,
gaiety and chattering in all my life. The kitchen
floor was simply covered with the shells of hard-
boiled eggs, radish tops and sandwich crumbs. It
was a grand party.

I was beginning to think it never would break
up, when at last, somewhere about two o'clock in
the morning, Matthew said he ought to be getting

back home. This gave Dab-Dab, who wanted to
get the kitchen cleaned up before breakfast-time,
a chance to shoo the family off to bed. The Doctor,
Matthew and I went into the study.

' 'Ow are you gettin' on with the book, Doctor?'
asked the cats'-meat-man.

'Well, Matthew,' said John Dolittle, 'not as fast
as I would like. But I'll be all right now that
Stubbins is taking over the patients for me. You
heard about that? Isn't it splendid? What would
I have done without him?'

'But listen, Doctor,' I said. 'You won't sit up too
late, will you? You'll have plenty of time to work
in the morning now, you know.'

'Time, Stubbins?' said he, a strange dreamy look
coming into his eyes. 'Time! If I'm successful with
my book and my experiments I'm going to make
time for everybody — for all the world!'

'I'm afraid I don't quite understand, Doctor,' I
said.

'Why — er — life,' said he — 'long life; perhaps
everlasting life. Think of it, Stubbins, to live as
long as your own world lives! That's what they're
doing up there in the Moon, or they will do it —
some of them — I'm sure. If I can only find the
secret!'

He sat down at his big desk and turned up the
wick of the whale-oil reading-lamp. There was a
slight frown on his face.

'That's it —' he muttered, 'if I can only *find* it.
All my life I've never had time enough. It's getting to be the same with most people now. Life
seems to grow busier every day. We are always
rushing, afraid we won't have time enough — to

do all the things we want to – before we die. But the older we grow the more worried we get. Worried! Worried that we won't get what we want done.'

He suddenly turned around in his chair and faced us both.

'But if we never grow old?' he asked. 'What then? Always young. All the time we want – for everything. Never to have to worry again about time. History tells us that philosophers, scientists before me, have always been seeking this thing. They called it "The Fountain of Youth", or some such name. Whenever an explorer found a new world he always heard some legend among the natives, some story of a wonderful spring or something whose waters would keep men for ever young. But they were all just – just stories and nothing more. But there in the Moon I have seen it. Creatures living on and on – in good health. That's the thing I'm working for – to bring everlasting life down to the Earth. To bring back peace to humanity, so we shall never have to worry again – about Time.'

He turned back to his desk as though he had a new thought he wanted to make a note of.

'I'm just going to see Matthew down to the gate, Doctor,' I said. 'Now *please* don't work too late.'

The cats'-meat-man and I stepped out into the garden. On our way round the house to the front, we had to pass the study window. We both stopped and gazed in a moment. John Dolittle was already writing away furiously. The little reading-lamp with its green glass shade threw a soft light on his serious, kindly face.

'There 'e is,' whispered Matthew, 'workin' away.
Ain't it like 'im? Tryin' to set the world to rights?
Well, it takes all kinds. . . . You know, Tommy,
me, I never seemed to 'ave time to bother about
settin' the world to rights. The world was always
tryin' to set me to rights – if yer know what I
mean. . . . Everlastin' life! Ain't it like 'im? D'yer
think 'e'll ever find it, Tommy?'

'Yes, Matthew,' I whispered back, 'I believe he
will. He has always succeeded in anything he's
set his heart on, you know.'

'Humph!' muttered the cats'-meat-man. 'Yus, I
wouldn't wonder but what you're right, Tommy.'

And silently we walked away through the
darkness towards the gate.

THE END

# Afterword

WHILE the *Doctor Dolittle* books
have continued to sell millions of copies in more
than a dozen languages around the world, ironi-
cally in the United States, where this world-
renowned story of the doctor who learned to speak
the animal languages was first published, the
books had been out of print for more than a
decade.

When it was decided to reissue the *Doctor
Dolittle* books in the United States, the editors
were faced with a challenging opportunity and
decision. In some of the books there were certain
incidents depicted that, in the light of today's
sensitivities, were considered by some to be dis-
respectful to ethnic minorities and, therefore,
perhaps inappropriate for today's young reader.
In these new editions this issue is addressed.

The problem that the editors faced was whether
or not to delete or rewrite portions of the *Doctor
Dolittle* stories. Publishers rightfully believe that
it is their job to publish a writer's work, not to act
as censors. Because the author is no longer living,
it was impossible to obtain his permission to

make changes. The *Doctor Dolittle* stories are, moreover, classics of children's literature, and on principle one can make a strong argument that one should not tamper with the classics.

Yet times have changed. Is it appropriate to leave the *Doctor Dolittle* books exactly as written and stand on principle at the expense of our obligation to respect the feelings of others? Should future generations of children be denied the opportunity to read the *Doctor Dolittle* stories because of a few minor references in one or two of the books that were never intended by the author to comment on any ethnic group, particularly when the references are not an integral or important part of the story? What should our response be when there is widespread disagreement among well-meaning parents, librarians and teachers as to the proper action to take?

To change the original could be interpreted as censorship. Then again, so could a decision to deny children access to an entire series of classics on the basis of isolated passing references. These were the difficulties faced when trying to decide whether or not to reissue the *Doctor Dolittle* books and whether or not it was appropriate to make changes in the original versions.

After much soul-searching the consensus was that changes should be made. The deciding factor was the strong belief that the author himself would have immediately approved of making these alterations. Hugh Lofting would have been appalled at the suggestion that any part of his work could give offence and would have been the first to have made the changes himself.

The message that Hugh Lofting conveyed throughout his work was one of respect for life and the rights of all who share the common destiny of our world. That theme permeates the entire *Doctor Dolittle* series.

Following the reissue of some of the *Doctor Dolittle* books in these new editions in the United States, it was decided that the same editions should also be made available to readers in Britain, through the publishers Red Fox. Only eight of the thirteen Doctor Dolittle books have been reissued in the United States, but Red Fox decided to publish the remaining five titles, too, and to revise them following the same principles applied in the revision of the other eight books.

And so we hope that Doctor Dolittle, Tommy Stubbins, Matthew Mugg, and the Doctor's animal family, are accessible again for a whole new generation of young readers to share their adventures.

# About the Author

HUGH LOFTING was born in Maidenhead, England, in 1886 and was educated at home with his brothers and sister until he was eight. He studied engineering in London and at the Massachusetts Institute of Technology. After his marriage in 1912 he settled in the United States.

During World War One he left his job as a civil engineer, was commissioned a lieutenant in the Irish Guards, and found that writing illustrated letters to his children eased the strain of war. 'There seemed to be very little to write to youngsters from the front; the news was either too horrible or too dull. One thing that kept forcing itself more and more upon my attention was the very considerable part the animals were playing in the war. That was the beginning of an idea: an eccentric country physician with a bent for natural history and a great love of pets . . . '

These letters became *The Story of Doctor Dolittle,* published in 1920. Children all over the world have read this book and the eleven that followed, for they have been translated into almost every language. *The Voyages of Doctor*

*Dolittle* won the Newbery Medal in 1923. Drawing from the twelve *Doctor Dolittle* volumes, Hugh Lofting's sister-in-law, Olga Fricker, later compiled *Doctor Dolittle: A Treasury*.

Hugh Lofting died in 1947 at his home in Topanga, California.